NCM PUBLISHING PRESENTS

Hidden RESENTMENT

STAR

AUTHOR OF BLOOD TIES

Hidden Resentment

Star

PUBLISHER'S NOTE :

This book is a work of fiction. Names, Characters, Places, and incidents
either are products of the author's imagination or are used fictitiously.
Any resemblance to actual events or locales or persons, living or dead,
is pure and entirely coincidental.

Copyright © 2015 Star
All Rights Reserved, including the right of reproduction
in whole or in part of any form.
ISBN: 978-0692408193
Library of Congress Catalog Card Number: in publication data.
Hidden Resentment
Written by: Star
Edited by: David Good, The Editing One
Text Formation: Write On Promotions
Cover Design and Layout: TSP Creative Design
Printed in the United States of America

Dedication

Giving all honor to God first.
I then would like to shout out
the NCM Publishing family, you guys rock!
To my dedicated husband and my children, One Love.

Contents

Chapter One		1
Chapter Two		11
Chapter Three		23
Chapter Four		31
Chapter Five		41
Chapter Six		51
Chapter Seven		61
Chapter Eight		73
Chapter Nine		77
Chapter Ten		91
Chapter Eleven		97
Chapter Twelve		109
Chapter Thirteen		119
Chapter Fourteen		131
Chapter Fifteen		133
Chapter Sixteen		143
Chapter Seventeen		151
Chapter Eighteen		157
Chapter Nineteen		161

Chapter One

can't stand this place! It is a roach infested dirty mess! The walls are dirty as hell and the floors are hideous. Mama don't give a damn though. She make me stay here anyway. She claim staying here, I am closer to school. I know that is a bunch of bull. It is my Aunt Tina's house so she don't see the harm in it. Even I realize she do not have any consideration for Aunt Tina's health, and the fact that she have two kids of her own to take care of. Not to mention that Aunt Tina's own kids took full advantage of her staying sick all the time. Drugs were the only thing that smothered mama's mind. Aunt Tina did not mind me being here, but as far as her health goes, I can notice that some days are worse than others but her attitude pretty much remain the same. I don't know what is wrong with her, but I figure it is something serious."

Let the story begin. Although I hated Aunt Tina's house, I loved her and her kids. My Aunt Tina was the sweetest lady one could ever meet. My cousin Shalese and Calvin were her only two kids. Shalese was a grade behind me, I was in the tenth at the timeand she was a freshman. Calvin was only eleven with a diehard passion for football.

While I Stood in the kitchen washing dishes, I looked around and told myself that I could not wait until I was grown and on my own. That was one good quality about my mama, she was a damn neat freak. One quality I didn't mind rubbing off on me. My father's name always left a sour taste on my tongue, because he was the sole reason mama was strung out on that outer space ship.

thanks a lot for doing my dishes." Shalese said. "Dag it is your night isn't it, oh well! You're late anyway. Where have you been?" "I was over Gerome's house." "Oh! I replied." "Shut up Stacie where's my mother at?" "I guess in her room, I don't know! Hey Shalese are you trying to go to the skating rink this weekend? I hear Jay and Tony is having a party up there." "Oh heck yeah count me in!" Shalese said. "Wait a minute are you talking about Jay and Tony in the 12th grade?" "Yeah Girl!" "Wow and since when is Stacie interested in boys!" "Shut up silly, I'm not gay nor am I blind!" "If you say so, I could of figured it was one or the other." Shalese said laughing. "I'll ask Aunt Tina before we go to school in the morning if we can go." "Aright, that's a bet."

In comes Cal with his big mouth. "And where do y'all think y'all going this weekend? Without giving us time to respond, he continued. "So y'all just gonna leave your boy hanging, what about my game?" "Boy we will be there." I said. Cal could be pretty annoying at times but I loved him to death, and the passion he had for the game was immaculate. I even enjoyed watching him play. He definitely had

Shalese and I went to her room to get our things ready for school the next day. Shalese insisted that I called her room my own, but that wasn't how I felt. I could not wait to be able to call something my own. The room was the one place I had to keep clean! The roaches were regular guest, but since I kept the room clean not too many of them camped out there.

I wanted to suggest that Aunt Tina bomb, but I did not want to hurt her Feelings or offend her. Come on, it didn't take a rocket scientist to know that roaches are just plain nasty. "Hey Stacie what are you wearing?" "I don't know Lese." "You can look through my stuff if you want too." Shalese offered. "Thanks cuz!" Shalese always had my back on the gear tip. "I will pick out something tomorrow after school, I am to tired right now. I missed the 49 bus so I ended get some rest." "Alright cuz, goodnight. Oh Lese did you set the alarm?" "Yeah it's set."

As I lay there I went deep into thought. Everything I had, I practically stole or borrowed it from Shalese. Shalese and Cal was lucky enough to have a good dad, he was just a bastard to Aunt Tina. He supplied all their needs and gave them monthly allowances. My father on the other hand was a piece of shit. He not only had my mama strung out on drugs but this nigga was now an on the strip, want to be pimp. I hadn't seen him in a year of Sundays. Screw a month of them. Oh well, off to sleep I went. A while later my sleep was rudely interrupted, Shalese's damn cell phone rung. I looked up at the clock and became even more pissed. It was 12:45 A.M. "What the hell, Shalese who is that? "With the sound of sleep in her voice she managed to say it was Davon.

Who in the world is Davon? I thought to myself. Being sleepy had me discombobulated. Then it came to me! The only Davon I was familiar with, was the older guy who hung out across the court. I definitely second guess that! "Hell no!" I said to myself. Shalese hot tail was way faster than I was. The winch started screwing in the seventh grade. Where they do that at! Boys really did not enthuse me yet, perhaps they never will. So I thought. Although I thought Tony and Jay were the jump-off, I could not imagine being with them. I noticed my attraction normally leaned toward the older guys. Most older guys who were half decent wouldn't give me the time of day because of my age. But I wasn't in any rush. I had already mastered the art of being horny, so I could care less. Not to mention my low self-esteem, that was a major factor for me. I barely ever felt like the cute one. I never thought that any guy could be attracted to me. I was about five feet, four inches tall. My skin, a caramel brown complexion and I was as bony as a toothpick. The one thing I did have was gorgeous hair and thanks to my own skills and expertise, it was always the bomb.

him tomorrow Gal-ee!" Shalese finally answered the phone. "Hello, I'm in the bed why wussup?" I pretended to fall back to sleep all the while I was being nosy ease dropping. I heard Shalese hot behind tell Davon to meet her at the back door.

It was such a shame, a descent woman like Aunt Tina with a slut for a daughter. In my opinion Aunt Tina was very naive. There was no way in hell she didn't know the things that Shalese was doing. All the signs were there. The way she dressed, her phone conversations and all. At times I didn't know whether I was jealous of my cousin, or was I really the miss goody two shoes. My mama was a darn mess! She was so strung out, that at times she couldn't even remember my name. My mama's addiction hurt me so bad. Although she wasn't the woman I remembered as a little girl I still loved her to death. When I was really young I could remember my mom being a pretty tan bone lady, with nice straight shoulder length hair. Radiant was an understatement. Mama was so beautiful, smooth, and she always had a fly fashion sense. I wish I could say she had the same great taste in men as she did in her clothes. Her taste in men was dog awful. I didn't recall every chain of events to make mama start using, but some things were unforgettable.

One night in particular, I was woke up out of my sleep by mama in a frantic mess. She told me to hurry and come on we were going to Aunt Tina's house. She was crying and had blood all over her shirt and hands. Seeing that made me cry and become frantic as well. I was so scared I grabbed mama's hand, and my shoes telling mama to come on let's run! Mama gave me this terrified look and we did just as I said, run! I later found out that when mama came home that night she caught my father having sex with another woman in their bed. Mama snapped and stabbed both of their butts up. Mama was lucky, she didn't spend a day in jail.

For one thing, they did not press charges, and when the state did pick it up her lawyer was able to get her acquitted. As beautiful as one who was going to put up with her bull. Basically brain washing her to believe she was the one with the problem. Unfortunately, like a desperate woman she just wanted to be loved by a man. That there was a bunch of crap. I will never understand it. I think at times that could be the reason I have such a nasty attitude toward guys in general. Of course I'm human so I think cute boys exist. I just don't see me being a damn slave to a man.

As far as my thoughts were from Shalese, I quickly refocused on her. I laid there tripping off Shalese. It was one o'clock in the morning and she was jumping up to a nigga's beat! I watched her out of the corner of my eyes as she got out of bed to put on a thong and a mini skirt. I thought that was the nastiest mess in the world. She was just with a dude a few hours ago and then she had the audacity to put some thongs on her funky ass! PEW! Shalese was like my little sister so I decided to have a one on one with her as soon as possible. The crap she doing was not cool! Some nights I would lay there and wonder why my life had to be so crappy and rotten. My father was missing in action which was cool with me, because I did not see life being any better for me with him around. Not the type of person he was, he made his own life a living hell! Mama was doing so good when we came to live with Aunt Tina after the stabbing.

Somehow my father manipulated his way right back in her life! The next thing I knew, mama's whole persona had changed. Her and Aunt Tina would argue and that was not Aunt Tina, so I knew something was up. Eventually Aunt Tina put her out. A lot of times I felt so alone so I looked forward to the little stuff. For a while I went through day to day thinking that nobody wanted me, or couldn't nobody see me for that matter. Until one day this boy actually showed some interest in me. I thought he was crazy, but from that day forward I started a diary and I wrote in it everyday. I couldn't wait until the next year because I would be legally grown.

care of my school business. Finally some sense kicked in somewhere and she brought me here to Aunt Tina's house for a second time. It had been about two years and that was where I had been ever since.

The alarm clock rung and I dreaded the thought of getting out of bed. I tossed and turned for most of the night, worrying about Shalese. Hoping and praying she would come back safely. I did not trust the guy Davon because word on the street was that he was a snake. Plus he was too damn old to be fooling around with my cousin! Both, Shalese and I were up and getting ready for school. "Shalese meet me after school, come straighthome I need to talk to you." "Okay!" Shalese replied. "Oh but wussup?"

"I'll tell you later Lese just be careful!" "Aright see you later. " The whole day in school I was unable to focus, I did no work at all. I practically wrote in my diary all day. Hearing that, could you believe my major was actually nursing. I should have been taking things a bit more serious! The fact that I didn't have much too look forward to, did not allow me to put all my effort into anything. Things like going to the skating rink on Saturday made me smile. Things that most teens do on the regular basis. After Saturday it would be back to nothing.

Finally school was over, but it seemed much quicker than normal. Thankfully it was, because by the time I got home, what felt like piss running down my legs was actually blood. I was so humiliated and embarrassed trying to figure out if anyone could see the blood stain between my legs. I wrapped my hoodie around my waist and hurried home.

Aunt Tina was a lot different from my mama. She would always keep the bathroom closet packed with pads and tampons. She had everything a woman would need, and I was grateful for that. Unlike my mama, I would have to use toilet paper to make a pad. Can you believe she showed me how to do it. And when she did she was a hated Aunt Tina's house. However, the roaches, the clutter, and the ghetto people made it hard to love. I finally made it home and the bathroom door was shut.

"Boom, Boom, Boom!" I knocked on the bathroom door. Only to find my cousin Calvin behind it singing. "Come on Cal I really have to go!" "I'm coming!" He said in his singing voice. Now Cal was a funny dude, he came running out laughing and still singing. "It stinks in there, cause my poop is in the air!" "Ha-ha very funny Cal, Move!" When I finally got in the bathroom my pants were soaked. It was so nasty, I threw away my clothes. Aunt Tina hadn't gotten in from work and Shalese didn't get in from school yet. I felt miserable. In times of mother nature, such as that moment, I wished I had my mom around and in her right frame of mind. With Cal about to go to football practice I would have the house to myself for at least thirty minutes or better.

I took a hot shower and then decided to go ball up in bed. The cramps were kicking my butt! Uncomfortable had to be an understatement. Uncomfortable and all I ended up getting up and writing in my diary. "Dear diary today was the most embarrassing day of my life! Can you say PERIOD!........It came unexpectedly at school. To top it off, my bloody cherry was thumping. I was having a horny spell. Ugh! Maybe I should let somebody pop this cherry, then life wouldn't be so bad!" I went on and wrote all of my feelings and by the time I finished I did not know where my life was headed. I was more lost at that point than ever before. As I closed my book I heard the front door close.

Shalese walked in the room and witnessed my frustration. "Are you okay Stase?" "Yeah I'll be, it's my menstrual." "Oh I totally understand!" "Look cuz I love you to death and I don't want to see anything happen to you. These different guys that you're dealing with aren't cool." "And why would you say that Stacie? Gerome will not find out, he's my school boyfriend but at home a girl still self-respect and what other people may label you as. Lese I know I cannot tell you what to do and I'm not trying to, but I want you to be careful! And Lese along with being careful you have to take your hygiene seriously." "Aww my big cousin love me!" "Of course I love you crazy! By the way did you sleep with Davon last night?" "Not really!" "And what in the heck does that mean?" "I gave him some head, now you happy!" My eyes got as big as Sponge Bob square pants. Without words I just stood there. Before I could say anything Shalese pulled out 2 one hundred dollar bills then said, "And this here is for our outfits for Saturday." Shalese started laughing and said, " But your cuz is gonna need you to hook her hair up though." I was still speechless but impressed at the same time. Damn, she must be good at what she do! I thought. Oh well, I wasn't about to turn down a free outfit. Shalese was on her way down the steps and I called her back.

"Stase I get that you love me and is concern about me but this here....... I been doing it for a long time. Way before you came and it's been working for me. Cuz please." "Hey that's not what I called you for, we only have two days left before Saturday. When are we going to the mall is what I want to know." We laughed so loud it was ridiculous. "Since tomorrow is Friday let's go tomorrow after school." "I'm in." I replied. "You know you gonna have to teach me your skills right!" Funny as it all was, I think I was dead serious. "Alright Stase I'm going downstairs to do my homework and look at some TV." "Okay I'll be up shortly."

I could not stand the thought of her getting hurt, but the only thing I could really demand of her was to be careful. Although me and Lese were only one grade apart in school, I was actually two years older than her. After a nap I was able to pull myself together, but when I woke up things were unsettling. I heard fussing and a lot of noise coming from the kitchen. I jumped up and ran down the steps. On the way toward the kitchen was when I heard Shalese screaming. The first thought that came to mind was that some girls face choking her. I yelled for him to get the hell off of my cousin. The nappy headed bastard kept choking her. He paid me no mind. When I noticed Lese gasping like she was on her last breath, I knew I had to do something and I had to do it quick.

I grabbed the 2 by 4 Aunt Tina had by the stove and whaled on his behind. I managed to get a good shot at his head. That stopped him dead in his tracks! Shalese started to panic when she saw the blood running down his face from his head. Her silly butt called the damn police! Davon hogged tailed out of the house! His last words were I'm gonna get you bitches! When the police came I left it all up to Shalese to tell what happened, because truthfully I did not know anything! I walked in on the end, that was my story and I was sticking to it. I overheard her telling the police that she was scared he would come after her again. She said the reason Davon hit her was because she didn't want to have oral sex with him. I didn't know what in the hell to believe because her story didn't quite make since! If the story about last night was true, why would he in turn whoop on her for not giving him head today? *"Oh well, it's over now."* That's what I thought to myself.

Just as the police was pulling off Aunt Tina was walking through Spring Ct. While Shalese was talking to the police I was in the house straightening things back up. It was a good thing I did, because by the time Aunt Tina came in everything seemed to be normal. Not really taking Davon's threat seriously to heart, we went on to make plans for tomorrow like we started. Her being scared of him all of a sudden was a whole different story, but whatever!

Chapter Two

When Aunt Tina came in she was in a different mood. She actually sat downstairs, laughed, and joked with Shalese and I. For starters she asked us how our day was, then she went on to tell us how much better she had been feeling. We talked about Calvin's game and she insisted on being there. She said she would not miss her baby's game for the world. That shocked me and Shalese. Aunt Tina gave me and Shalese a hug before she went into the living room to wait on Cal to come home. The way Aunt Tina was acting kind of scared me. I didn't know whether it was a good thing or bad thing because this was definitely out of the normal for her. I have to admit I liked her that way a lot better. As for Shalese she stayed far away. Of course she was afraid of all her funky skeletons coming out of the closet. Aunt Tina didn't mind her having a cell phone for whatever reason, but her phone held all her slutty intentions. After Shalese and Davon's escapade I started to bleed heavier. I was trying to wait for the right time but I had questions for her butt that just couldn't wait any longer!

"Aright Aunt Tina I'm bleeding like a dog, I'm gonna go lay down." "Okay sweetie, while you're up there get two Pamprin off of my dresser, that will ease your discomfort." "Okay love you Auntie." "Love you too Stase."

As I laid there, I heard Cal come in, that was a relief. Our family wasn't big at all so we were all we had. Shalese was in the bathroom

Aunt Tina. When she finally came out of the bathroom I was more than furious. In a demanding but low tone I questioned her. "What the heck was that about Lese?" "Stacie did'nt you hear what I told the police, well that's what happened." "I don't understand, you was just with him last night!" "Exactly!" Shalese replied. "So Stase where are we meeting tomorrow?" "I'll meet you at the westside shopping center, we can go to Security Sqaure Mall from there." "Aright that's cool with me." Shalese replied. This was only like my fifth time coming on my period and it always seem to shut my world down! fortunately I would only stay on for three days, and compared to everyone else I was a late bloomer. Most girls my age had already had their period.

I fell asleep that night, I didn't eat, I didn't do any homework, and I didn't give a care. The next morning when the alarm went off I contimplated not going to school but I got up anyway. Instead of going to school I detoured to the library. I was actually headed for school until I heard those same boogee ass broads from yesterday loud talking. They put my embarrassing moment on blast. That was not okay. Sometimes I wished that the girls who seemed to have everything could walk a week in my shoes. Maybe then they wouldn't be so insensitive.

As angry as I was I could not imagine fighting about everything. I figured it was not only a waste of time but a waste of energy too. To top it off I was not at all a fighter. I wouldn't say I was a punk but I did'nt know if I even knew how to fight. That mess that happened the night before with Shalese and Davon, that was just my natural instinct that kicked in. I wasn't fittin to see my cousin loose her life in front of me. Stuff like that was for the birds and I damn sure couldn't fly. After school, Lese and I met at the library like we agreed. Today was a classic sweatpants, addidas, and tee shirt day for me. Comfortable was my m.o. Shalese on the other hand did not have those days. Of course she wore the four inch pumps with the she could get paid for. So taking fashion tips from her was a given. In the mall I took Shalese's guidence as far as my outfit was concerned. I didn't know how to do sexy all that great. Messing with her my skinny didn't matter.

Leaving the mall my confidence was sky rocket high. I was so excited and looking forward to tomorrow. After we left the mall we stopped passed the hair store. Shalese had the gift to gab so while she occupied the owner, I stole everything we needed. On the bus ride home Shalese and I shared a few inner secrets. I told her I was thinking about having sex. She found that to be so amusing. "Stacie...you turn down everybody who even speak to you, how are you suppose to get laid!" "You funny Shalese, I aint that dar-gon outdated!"

"I tell guys I don't have a phone and they give me their number. For the most part I never run into them again anyway so it does not matter if I call or not." Shalese bust out laughing. "What the hell....... and you are suppose to be the oldest! Stacie that was the lamest crap I done heard yet! Stase you have to step your game up cuz foreal!" My lame tail just sat there grinning not saying a darn word. Deep down inside I knew my cousin just spoke a true statement. It was like a half a year away before I turned eighteen and not only have I not had sex yet, I didn't really have a career goal in mind. Although I went to Edmondson High School for nursing, I was not sure if that's what I truly wanted to do. I didn't know if I was getting older or finally gainning a conscious, because it was eating me up that I had stole all of our hair supplies. Normally that was not the case at all, I would not have thought twice about it. "Stase how are you wearing your hair?" "You know what......it depends on how the outfit look on me when I put it on. I was thinking about doing the Malaysian hair. However if the look requires something different than different it will be. How about you and your head Lese?" "Girl I just want something simple, you can give me a wrap and I'll be good." "Cool that won't take me no time."

me and shalese for what we saw. Cal was sitting in the front seat of Davon's car. "Oh boy!" I mumbled.

Now one thing was for sure, we all knew Davon wasn't any good, but to have anything to do with Cal was more disturbing. It was just yesterday I busted his damn head! "Stase let's go around back I don't trust Davon." "Shalese are you freakin kidding me, HELL NO! Do you realize Cal is in his car! NO yo ass can go around back but I want my lil cousin outta his dam car!" Shalese actually left me and went around back.

For a minute my heart dropped but I walked toward the car anyway. Lucky for me Cal got out of the car as I approached it. Davon punk behind pulled off. That spoke volumes. I knew it had to be more to the story than Shalese was telling. "Cal why were you in his car?" "Oh nothing he was asking me about the game!" "And since when do he care anything bout your games? Look Cal what is really going on?" "Stacie I told you nothing!" I did not buy his story for a second. "Calvin yesterday Davon did some mean things to Shalese please stay away from him." "Well Stase that's probly because she did something mean to him, Davon is a nice guy, he's not like that." "Just listen to me please Cal, at least until all this blow over." I stormed into the house and who was standing there looking stupid..... Shalese. I wanted to smack the hell out of her. I was just about sick of the drama. "Why did you freakin leave me to deal with that by myself, that was a selfish coward move Shalese!" He is your little brother you know! Suppose I would have just turned my back on you yesterday huh!"

"Stacie I am sorry, but I really am afraid of what he might do to me!" "Shalese what is done is done we whooped his butt, but life goes on! The next time I tell you to come on you betta get unscared. I was scared too yesterday but I wasn't gonna let him hurt you!" "Besides that shit wasn't even that serious. "Shalese facial expression didn't agree with the words that were coming out of my mouth. "Shalese

As usual Aunt Tina was barricaded in her room, she didn't have a clue what was going on with her kids and the house looked like shit! For the most part the house was just messy. Cal never took his clothes and shoes upstairs. Aunt Tina's mail sat in piles everywhere, and anything that was Shalese's could be found anywhere in the house. Shalese and I were able to take the angry faces off our face. Then we went in the room and started our hair. I did Shalese hair first since she knew exactly what she wanted. I gave her a mean wrap with a slanted bang. After finishing her hair I was too tired to do my own. Instead of going to bed I decided to go sit on the front stoop. I called it a stoop cause it was too big to be a step. The night air was brisk and for it to be September, Spring Ct. was still live like it was July.

Spring Ct. is a court located in the Perkins Holmes projects. Spring Ct. happened to be one of the more settled courts at the time. Besides the old drunks and the children, there wasn't too much to it. Now the court across from Sping CT. was a bad dream waiting to happen. I normally didn't find it appealing to sit on the stoop because of all the shooting that went on. Our court hardly ever caught any of the action but bullets do fly. I sat out there and laughed at the girls next door. They weren't to fond of me and I could not tell you why. Like I said before, I was bony and didn't have a lot of anything. My hair yes....it was always fly but after that I was the average seventeen year old, maybe with a little less.

Aunt Tina came to the door frantically looking for Calvin. I told her that he should have been in the house. She told me she had already looked all over the house for him and he was not in there. I got up and went inside with Aunt Tina and she was right. Cal wasn't no where to be found. Damn, he must of left out when I was doing Shalese hair. I thought to myself. I wondered if I should tell Aunt Tina what had been going on. Once I thought about it a little bit longer, I decided that it was definitely not a good idea. I did not want anything to mess with her health.

·

him! Stacie, the last time I had a bad dream about somebody it was my brother, your Uncle Kelly. Honey I didn't do anything and today my brother is dead. It could of been a sign."

My eyes got big, I didn't know what to say. I just called for Shalese. "Shalese!" Shalese came nrnning. It was like she could hear the fear in my voice. "Hey Ma what's wrong?" "It's Cal, I told you we have to find Cal." Aunt Tina said. When Aunt Tina opened the back door Cal was running toward the house. "Calvin Jermain Lewis get your narrow behind up in this dam house! Are you crazy, Where were you? You are only eleven years old not twenty-one! And that dam game........you aint going!" "Ma please.....I'm sorry!" Calvin replied.

I never saw Aunt Tina so verbal and upset. I almost wanted to clap my hands because I thought it was about darn time. Maybe I should tell her about the Davon situation, not all of it just the part when his ugly ass put his hands on my cousin. But that mean I might as well tell on myself too. I was far from innocent but some things were just completely out of my league. Aunt Tina then turned to Shalese and asked her about the last time her father brought them some money. Her initial thought was to take any money Cal had. She was heated with him. Shalese began to stutter and shit........" Ummmm I-- I -thin--think it was last Monday, but Ma that money might be gone he only brought us twenty dollars a piece. Then I went to put my two cents in it! "Shalese I thought.......was all I got to say.

Shalese shut me up quick! "No that was the time before." I didn't even get to say anything, I just shook my head. I guess that was my que. Was my cousin a totally different person than she led the people in this house to believe. Not much is making since anymore. Granted Shalese would share when her dad came and brought her money! What I thought was funny, was that I never saw him when he was suppose to had came. Oh but the funniest of them all, was that he only came when Aunt Tina was at work. I was beginning to think they were all lies. "I'm going to bed yall, goodnite." I said. It

Poor Cal, he can't even play his season opener. I don't blame her though, she was scared shitless.

Early the next morning I woke up to do my hair. Most weekends I would sleep in until at least ten, this morning I was up by eight. For a very odd reason I could not sleep. When I got up I couldn't even start my hair right away. I sat on the side of the bed with an uneasy feeling. I glanced over at Shalese and she was still in a deep sleep. For the life of me I could not shake the feeling. I went out in the hallway and peeped in Aunt Tina's room and Cal's room, they both were asleep. Since everything seemed to be normal I went back in the bedroom and started my hair.

I had made up my mind, I decided to go with the Malaysian hair with the wave. Plus that style wouldn't take me all day to do. My mother was on my mind when I got up this morning. However, because of her track record I quickly discarded my feelings. Aunt Tina knew how to get in touch with my mama but I rarely asked her too. My hair was just about done and everyone was still sleeping. I took advantage of the peace and quiet. Instead of going to eat breakfast I pinned my hair up and laid across my bed. A little while later I heard Cal come out of his room.

"Cal, is that you?" "Yeah, hey Stase." "Cal are you excited this morning about your big game? Oh wait, did Aunt Tina change her mind?" "And you know this man!" Cal said all pumped. We both laughed. Cal was so funny, he came right in our room and sat on Shalese. "Get up Shalese, Gerome is on the phone." Shalese popped up like bread from a toaster. Then Cal said, "sike just joking." Shalese was mad at Cal for a minute but she quickly got over it when she realized, it was Saturday. "Hey Stacie you did your hair huh! So I see you decided to go with the Malaysian wave!" "Yeah guurl! I'm ready for this fun filled day." "I know that's right!" Shalese said. Aright yall I have to go get ready, the coach will be here in a little bit." "Already Cal!" I said. "Yeah we're going out for breakfast. Then from there we are going to the field to go over our plays."

I don't know, Our schedule is determined by what time the team before us get of the field. I'll call you're phone from Coach Dre's phone. Oh yeah and tell Ma to be there or be sqaure!" "Boooy you dumb!" I said. "Stase while Mama is sleep let's go to Crazy Johns and get some pizza." "Pizza, what the hell!" "Come on Stacie please!" "Ok whateva!"

Today definitely wasn't a normal Saturday. Usually Shalese, Cal, and myself would wake up around ten and be the loudest things in the projects. Aunt Tina would yell at us at least three times for us to keep the noise down. I can remember one morning we were so loud that Aunt Tina locked our behinds out back. Huh, I won't fall for that one again. Shalese and I really walked to Crazy Johns. Me and her played around and lost track of time. We ran into Tony at Crazy Johns and we were in awe. Tony was one of the seniors having the party tonight and he was hot as hell! What a coincidence I thought to myself. Jay was a looker too, he just wasn't my type. He was one of those loud guys. Tony was a pretty quiet boy. When Tony spoke to us, we spoke as if our damn hearts dropped in our stomachs. Further more, I couldn't believe he even spoke to us. Shalese was a pro, I didn't know how she did it.

When Shalese looked at the phone it was 1:30. "Oh shoot Stase we gotta hurry back!" Thank goodness Crazy Johns wasn't that far from the projects. It was located right before downtown on Baltimore Street, but we still had to walk. Baltimore street was known for the infamous strip joints. They smothered most of the block. Those and arcades. Which is why it was labled the hot block. Shalese always joked about being eighteen so she could strip two nights a week. The more and more she said it, the more serious she began to sound. Shalese phone started ringing.

"Hello, Hey Cal wussup?" "Hey Lese, my game start at two thirty." "Dag Cal, why are you just calling, you should have been called and told us!" "Sorry Lese I forgot." "Okay we'll be there." "I already text Mommy Shalese so she might be on her way already." "Aright Cal." "That was Cal, Stase we have to hurry up because we only have fourty five more minutes until game time." "Well dam!" I said. "I know, right!" Me and Shalese put a little pep in our step to hurry up home. When we got there we both went into the bathroom at the same time. I used the sink and she used the shower. We put our clothes on and headed to the game.

The game was packed out! Parents were there hooting and hollering pumping their kids up. Aunt Tina was nowhere to be found. That was odd because even though Cal made Aunt Tina mad last night, she wouldn't have missed his game for the world. Shalese tried to assure me it was possible that she was just running late.

Somehow my gutt instincts said that something was wrong. I could feel it. It was kickoff time. Cal's team were the Warriors and their opponents were the Gators. I don't know what position Cal played but he was responsible for running the ball to get a touch down. I guess he was a ruuning back. I wasn't much of a football fan but there were a lot of hot guys on and off the field. Calvin's coach was the shit! That dude needed some toilet paper! He didn't look a day over twenty-five but I knew better. He had to be a little older than that. He had such a young and vibrant look. He was a brown skin dude with a regular hair cut. He rocked a gray colored sweatsuit with a blue stripe down the leg of the pants with some fresh blue and white nikes. "Wow! Is he really this fresh to coach football!" I said to myself. I really couldn't tell much about his built but everything seemed to be in shape.

The warriors had the ball and they were driving. The qaurterback passed the ball to Cal and that little boy took off like lightening. He was on the fifty, then the forty, down to the twenty, "TOCHDOWN WARRIORS!" The commentator said. When Cal ran off the field the coach gave him a high five. He was so excited. As the game went on the Warriors were winning, but the time was passinig and still no Aunt Tina. Shalese called her several times and got no answer. I wanted to leave and go find out what was going on, but I didn't want to alarm Cal.

It was the season opener and the first time they had ever won the opener in there little franchise history. I was sooo happy for Cal! Shalese and her big darn mouth, "GOOOOOO CALVIN!" The coach looked our way and laughed. Shalese and I seen eye to eye on a nice looking guy. But she would always take stuff a step further. She wanted us to go introduce ourselves. That girl was a true mess! Just as we approached him so did some other chick. "Oh well it was too late then, we were there." I thought. The coach turned to the chick and told her, to give him a minute then she walked off.

"Hi I'm Shalese, Calvin's sister." "And I'm Stacie Calvin's cousin." I said cutting her off. Then of course there was loud mouth again AND YOUR COACH.......! "Dag Shalese the man is right here." "I am coach Dre." I smiled. Coach Dre huh, I said to myself. He caught my smile and he smiled back. Then we were rudely interrupted by the chick who went back and sat in the bleachers. "Alright ladies, yall have a good day." "You too." Shalese said. I said nothing, I just winked my eye at him. Don't ask me where that came from! I couldn't believe I just done some madness like that. The funny thing was, he caught the gesture and winked back. True, it was September but a sista body felt the heat. The chemistry was oh too natural.
Hidden Resentment, Bolding/ Page 27

I wanted to faint right there, but I had to keep my composer. Or else I would be the lame that Shalese said I was. Shalese asked Cal was he going to catch a ride home with us or was he hanging out with the team. He decided to hang out with the team. Which was cool with us. We thought he should've went to celebrate his first victory. As we were walking off, Cal came running back. "Stacie, Coach Dre told me to give you this, and oh yeah tell Ma to be sqaure." I opened the paper and dude's number was on it. "Thanks Cal, see you later." When did he manage to do that I wondered, cause the chick had not left his side. Maybe it was because Cal was going with him. You know, in case we needed to contact him.

Cal?" "Stacie, Stacie, Stacie....... Uuh cuz I told you, you wouldn't be able to see it if it was right in your face. And well I was right!" "Shut up Shalese!" Shalese laughed at me and then mumbled, "And you talk about getting laid." "So when are you gonna call him?" "I don't know, I can't act all pressed, duuuh! Now Shalese you should know that!" "Let's say you're not pressed, now when are you gonna call him?" "Maybe tomorrow, Lese I said I don't know! You are a dam hulk!" I said. Shalese did Aunt Tina ever text or call you back?" "Nope, and that is not like her, I am starting to get mad worried cuz. Now it was Shalese and I both with the uneasy feelings so we decided to go straight home. Maybe at home would be a sign of Aunt Tina and her where abouts.

I agreed with Shalese, this was not like Aunt Tina. She could always be found, unlike Lisa's junkie ass. Lisa is my mom, and yes I love her to death but I am also very angry with her. Shalese thought we were catching the bus but I told her let's flag down a cab. She went on to tell me that she would not have enough money to catch a cab, go to the party, and have a enough spending money. I reassured her that I had it. I let Shalese in on my rainy day fund that I had stashed away at home.

"Oh, so you been holding out on me huh!" "I wouldn't say that, it's just that everytime I get a little bit of money I put a little away in case of emergencies like right now. Finally we got a cab. The whole ride home Shalese was calling Aunt Tina's phone and neither time did she get an answer. When we arrived at the house I told Shalese to pay for the cab and I would give her the money back once we were inside. She did what she was told then we exited the cab.

Chapter Three

The sun was fading behind the clouds and that played a big role on my emotions at times. I didn't understand it, but it seemed like during the day my rotten life wouldn't seem so darn rotten! But when the night fell, it was like I had to fight off this depressing phase. I mean this was everyday like clockwork. Shalese's face became more weary as we got closer to the front door. The house was as quiet as a mouse. Shalese called out to Aunt Tina but Aunt Tina was not there. Shalese called Ms. Jackie to see if she had heard from Aunt Tina.

"Hello Ms. Jackie, this is Shalese, have you seen or heard from my mother?" "Shalese I have not talked to her today, but I spoke to her last night. That is when we made plans to go to the jazz festival tonight." " Shalese I'll call Mr. Richard and see if he heard from her and I'll be on my way over there. I might as well wait for her there." "Ok Ms. Jackie." "Shalese what did Ms. Jackie say?" "She have not spoke to her today. But she did speak to her last night about going to the jazz fest today. I also find it strange cause I did not know Mama and Mr. Richard still was in touch." "Well maybe that's it, she might have went shopping to find something to wear." "That would be an option just not today. She would not have gone shopping on Cal's first game day. She would not hurt him like that." "Yeah you got a point."

I rubbed Shalese on her back because when I looked at her, I could tell she was past worried. Tears started coming down her face and only one way to find out. We have to call the coach phone. Do you want to call him or do you want me too?" "Can you please Stacie." "Yeah." Shalese was really scared, she would never turned down the opportunity to call any guys phone. Dre's phone was ringing.

"High you doing coach, this is Stacie... Cal's cousin. Ummmm do you know if my aunt text or called your phone back earlier?" "I don't think so but hold while I check." "Okay." I responded. "Nope, she never text back. Stacie is everything okay?" "I don't know but can you not tell Cal anything yet! We cannot find my Aunt Tina." "Oh Wow!" "Okay I'll keep lil man busy, can I call you back on this number before I bring him home?" "Yeah that would be fine. Thanks a lot." "No problem sweetie."

Shalese started shaking her head. She practically already heard the conversation through the phone. Shalese when we came back from Crazy Johns how do you know Aunt Tina wasn't in her room?" "Did you go in there?" "Yes." Shalese said in a low tone. "I peeped in there and she wasn't in the bed. The weird thing was Mama's bed wasn't made up!" "Stacie she always makes her bed up!" Shalese began to cry harder. I told Shalese I would call some local hospitals and she should call her dad. Even though he never had Aunt Tina's best interest this was desperate measures.

I knew they had a pretty good relationship with him. Come to find out Shalese and Cal haven't seen their father in over eight months. She was lying about getting money from him for her and Cal. She also admitted to sleeping with guys to get the money she was bringing home. The real story bout Davon shocked me the most though! Yeah she did perform oral sex on him but he only gave her fifty dollars. When he went to the bathroom she took two hundred more. That's what the fight was about. She cried on my shoulder and told me how sorry she was for lying to me, and putting me in the middle of her drama. She confessed to me that her father wasn't around at all, but she never told Aunt Tina because she knew how sick she was.

won't say anything." I was stunned that the situation was even that deep that it was a secret. "Oh I - I won't!" "Mama has stage four cancer, the worst possible stage. We know her time is coming soon. I cut my father off because he left Mama in her time of need. This is why Mama stay in her room a lot. I didn't realize what was going on until I got a little older. I use to worship the ground my father walked on. Mama had cancer for six years. At one point it was in remission, but then two years ago it came back. This time it came back worse, it went to her brain."

Tears filled my eyes and my vision became blurry, but yet and still I tried to keep my composure for my cousin. "Wow poor Aunt Tina, I feel so bad for making her yell at us on Saturdays." "She really did need her rest and to think now that I was the cause of her missing any is messing me up." "Stase Mama love you do not do this to yourself! When we find her we can just tell her how much we love her too." "I will." A light came on in Shalese's head, then she said, "You know what, Mama got a small black book with other folks in it that she talk to. Stacie I be right back.

Shalese went upstairs and to Aunt Tina's room. Suddenly I heard a glass break followed by a loud scream. "Maaaaaaaaaaaaaaaa, Mama, Mama get up!" "Oh my God Shalese what's wrong!" I said to myself. In my heart I already knew but I could not pick myself up to get up those steps. I heard Shalese continue to cry out in agony.

"Mama Noooo, get up.......... You wasn't spose to go wit-out saying bye! Why you do this to meeeeeeee!" When I heard her say what am I suppose to tell Cal, Mama we can't live without you! Daddy aint SHIT! I hurried myself up there but not before I broke down crying and shaking. It was then, more than ever before that my cousin needed me. When I reached Aunt Tina's room I was stopped in my tracks. One reason was, I did not see Aunt Tina nor Shalese. Second of all the crying was coming from the other side of the bed, on the no no no no...........Aunt Tina! Why?" Shalese yelled, "Call the ambulance, call the ambulance NOW!" I ran back downstairs to get her phone and quickly dialed 911. Aunt Tina was gone, it wasn't no doubt in my mind. Once I got off of the phone I went back upstairs and sat next to Shalese. I held her so tight. Aunt Tina had very light skin that would bruise if you hugged her too tight. Her skin was blue at that point. The wait for the ambulance seemed so long when it was actually not long at all. When I heard them coming down the street I went downstairs to open the door. While I was down there I called the coach back.

"Coach is there anyway at all that Cal can stay with you tonight?" Uuuhhhh.... sure, is everything okay?" "No...No its not!" Still crying, I managed to say, "Aunt Tina is dead." "What, are you serious?" Is there anything I can do?" The coach asked. "Yes please take care of Cal for us tonight." Okay Stacie please call me later on tonight when everything is a bit more calm." "Of course I'll call you later." I let the paramedics in and they shot straight up the steps. I could hear Shalese saying in here, over here! Because Aunt Tina did not have a pulse, a heartbeat, nor was she breathing, she was instantly pronouced DOA. That simply meant dead on arrival. Therefore, because she was gone the police had to also come to the scene.

In turn, the situation had prolonged and wouldn't be over for a long while. They also explained to us that the coroner had to come get Aunt Tina's body. While Shalese had to soak all of this in, I got Aunt Tina's black address book and started calling people. There was no way we could deal with it alone. So I decided to call Ms. Jackie back. When she answered the phone she said, Shalese I'm two minutes away. I then said, "Ms. Jackie this is Stacie, Aunt Tina is gone......... The phone hung up in my ear and I did not have the strength to call her back. Not thinking at all, when she said she was two minutes away I should have just waited til she got there. I found a number with the name Lisa by it. I wasn't sure if it was my mother or someone else. The hell with it, is what I said to myself, as I decided to call the

"Um, hello is Lisa there?" "Who is this?" The man said, in his groggy voice. "This is Stacie, Tina's niece." The man placed me on hold and when the phone was picked back up it was a woman. This womans voice did not sound familiar at all. "Hello my name is Stacie, your name is in my Aunt Tina's phone book, is this Lisa?" "Young lady it's Mama to you, you don't know your own mothers voice?" For about sixty seconds I thought I was being pranked, then oddly I had a sigh of relief. To hear Mama's voice, it was pleasing to me but when I realized how ill she sounded my happiness faded instantly. "Mama you need to come over to Aunt Tina's house it's important." "Stacie c'mon what the hell is going on girl you messin up my high now?" At times I hated her ill mannered behind. I wanted to hang up the phone and not tell her ass nothing!

"Look Mama it's important something has happened to Aunt Tina, you gotta get over here now!" "Why didn't yo dumb ass just say dat in da first place!" Mama just added more pain to my heart and couldn't even help it. I always forgave my mother because I was always under the assumption it was the drugs that affected her actions. My mama needed help and I knew it. I could not stand the thought of Aunt Tina's body lying there lifeless for hours and we didn't know. Poor Shalese she could not stop crying. Ms. Jackie was a good friend to both Aunt Tina and my mother in high school. However as they got older they all went there seperate ways and did seperate things. Aunt Tina went on and got married, but then she took sick. Mama turned to the life of drugs. Ms. Jackie had her a couple of kids and remained the party goer. The fact that her and Aunt Tina had plans to hang out was quite the shocker.

When Ms. Jackie came in the house she called out for Shalese and I. I went down stairs to let her know what was going on. When I got down there Ms. Jackies eyes were already filled with tears and that did not make it any easier. "Stacie, baby tell me it's not true!" "Yes Ms. Jackie she is gone!" "What happen Stacie?" "Honestly I like her so we called you. Shalese went upstairs in her room to get her address book and there she was lying on the floor tangled in her

"Oh my goodness I just talked to her last night and she seemed fine." Ms. Jackie said. "Ms. Jackie did you know about her cancer?" "Honey your Aunt Tina's cancer went in remission years ago, are you saying that it came back?" "Yes ma'am, and this time she didn't want anyone to know. She told Shalese she was tired of fighting. The only reason she told Shalese was to prepare her for this. The last time she told everyone her husband abandoned her, my mom left; went and got hooked on drugs. She did not want to bother anyone else with her health. Aunt Tina also partially blamed herself for my mama getting hooked on drugs." "WHAT?" She feel like she was the oldest sister and since she took care of Mama for years she would always be responsible for her." "Oh Lord!" Ms. Jackie said.

The coroner had not come yet! It was 1:10 in the darn morning! This was something new to me so I didn't have a clue why the hell they took so long. Shalese had finally stopped crying but she sat there in complete silence until she thought about Cal. "My brother....... what are we gonna do?" In my mind there was no preparing for this. Then because of Shalese lying about the relationship with her dad, made things more troubling. Ms. Jackie sat there and waited with us. By that time it was 1:25, and guess who came bouncing in the door? I wish it was the damn coroner! It was Lisa! I was so disgusted with her. The look on Shalese's face was devastating. I could smell trouble

The first words that came out of that womans mouth were, "Ware my sisa at!" She was as high as a kite. It seemed like she got even higher to come over here. No one said a word. Even Ms. Jackie sat there in awe. Shalese was so mad she sat there and just lowered her head to the table. Then the woman went MAD! She started blurting out a whole heap of unecessary shit then. I tried my best to calm her down but before I could it was on and poppin.

child like. I don't think she believed what I said because she just stood there. "Stop playin this bullshit game girl ware is my SISA?" "GO THE HELL UPSTAIRS AND SEE DEN! Just stop getting on our dam nerves." I yelled. I never yelled at my mother before then. I always believed in respecting my elders no matter what. Mama stumbled up the steps. I was so sad for Shalese and yet so embarrassed for mama. Mama got up there and saw the paramedics just standing around not working on Aunt Tina and she flipped the heck out. When she saw Aunt Tina on the floor things began to register. "Not my SISA, she aint dead, who da hell they think they talking too. C'mon Sissy get up and show deese mutha sukas!" "Mama went over to Aunt Tina and tried to drag her across the floor. "GET UP SISSY!" I hurried up and got up those steps before Shalese did.

"Mama stop!............ Please let Aunt Tina rest!" "Nooooo She aint gone no ware! She right here dummy!" Mama was still pulling on her and it looked like a fire hydrant hit her. I didn't know what was worse her crying or her sweating. Shalese entered the room with rage in her eyes. "If you don't get off of my mother and get out, I will have you thrown out by the police!" I had never heard Shalese sound so angry and serious but in the lowest tone you could possibly imagine. "What did you say lil guurl!" Mama said. "You heard exactly what I said!" "Now leave!" I stood there and said not one word, Shalese had every right to say what she said. "My sisa laying over here dead cause of yall asses! I aint going no dam ware! If yall woudn't put her through so much she still be heeeya! Now make me leave!"

Shalese eyes started running again nonstop. She should not have to deal with this. I thought to myself. "Mama stop it! Now I am telling you to just get the hell out!" "If I leave you comin wit me!" "No I'm not just GEEET OUT!" "You know what Stacie FUCK YOU! My life turned into shit the day you were born, so fuck you!" "I hauled off and smacked the sweat off her face. Oh goodness I had just hit my mama! "Now get the fuck out, cause it's more where that met mama on the steps.

She didn't know how to approach mama; it had been so long. She wanted her to know things would be ok over time. UUUPS and there goes mama! "And who da hell is you?" "Lisa, it's Jackie." "Jackie Right?" Mama said. "Yeah girl it's me, Jackie Right." Mama damn near hugged the life out of Ms. Jackie. Ms. Jackie took her by the hand and went outside with her. The coroner finally arrived at two o'clock that morning. They took Aunt Tina's body but for me and Shalese that was just the beginning. For a long while Ms. Jackie, me, and Shalese sat and talked about Aunt Tina in her better days.

We had no idea how we were going to tell Cal, better yet what we would do and how? When Shalese confessed the truth about their dad she also told me that she had no dealings with his family either. It was 4:30 in the morning when Ms. Jackie left. As tired as I was there was no sleeping in my near future. At least that's what I thought. I was kind of too afraid to sleep. When I came back from locking the door Shalese was balled up on the couch drifting off to sleep. She needed me right then and I intended on being there every step of the way. I went upstairs and grabbed the first blanket I saw. I laid beside my cousin and put my arms around her determined not to let her go. Mourning for her mother and my aunt, we held each other tight and went to sleep.

Chapter Four

totally forgot to call the coach back last night. So that will be the first call I make this morning. I got Shalese cell phone off of the counter and it was dead. Once I found the charger I proceeded to make the call.

"Good morning Coach, is Calvin okay?" "Yes, sweetie he is fine, how are things over there?" "Quiet." I said. "I am so sorry to hear about your aunt." "Thanks for everything, how is Cal....I know I asked you that before but......" "No need to explain, I understand." "Umm, Coach you didn't tell him did you?" "Naw......but if you need me to I will." "Well, I thought it should probly be something me and his sister should do . Seems as though neither one of us is able to do it though, please be gentle." "I got you, as a matter of fact how about we tell him together, the three of us." "Wow you are awesome!" "Do you or your cousin need anything?" "Look Coach I'm not trying to be a bother to you, we are good." "First and for most, call me Dre and second of all, you will never be a bother to me.

"I know this probly is not the right time, but I would like to get to know you personally Stacie." "Okay if you say so Dre!" "I will be there in about an hour." Dre responded. Dag was I really that rude to him just now, I really do have to step my game up. I promised myself today I would try my best to hold up for Shalese and Cal. Shalese was tossing and turning out of her sleep. I went over to her and placed my hand on her shoulder.

a fool for asking her was she okay. She couldn't have been okay! I honestly thought better was an overstatement until she began to explain herself. "I thought no one could be better the day after their mother died. She told me how she was glad Aunt Tina didn't have to suffer anymore, and that Aunt Tina came in her dream and told her that she was ok.

As the day progressed it became very busy. Dre brought Cal home and Ms. Jackie came back over. I could not believe my eyes when even Lisa showed up. The kicker was, my mama being as sober as a new born baby. Cal took it really hard. I mean really hard! In turn, Shalese began to sob simultaneously. She could not take seeing Cal so heart broken. Although it was a sad day for us I managed to have two descent conversations. I couldn't believe it took for death to happen for me to start seeing a positive change in my life. After talking to Dre, I found out how interesting he was and how interested he was

My mama and I had a real one on one, I could tell Aunt Tina's death did a number on her. While we talked I noticed her inability to focus. I touched her leg and told her everything would be fine. When I said that a tear came down her face. She apologized to Shalese and I for all the pain she caused. Shalese and Cal were too young to do the funeral arrangements so Ms. Jackie and mama did them. The entire time all the way up to Aunt Tina's funeral mama was sober, at least when she came around she was. I was so proud of her.

After the third day Shalese and Cal's father showed up. Cal was too excited to, she could care less! Ultimately Shalese new the real deal. Somehow I convinced her to let it go and try to move forward. I think he had a change of heart as well because he came with his A game. He also asked them did they want to go with him. Lese really didn't want to go but it wasn't like she had to much of a choice. She was only fifteen. So because she was still a minor she had to go. Anthony who is Shalese and Cal's father agreed to let them stay in

Aunt Tina was very smart, she had a life insurance policy for a hundred thousand dollars along with a living will. She only wanted ten thousand spent on her funeral and she set aside fourty thousand a piece for Shalese and Cal. My aunt even left me ten thousand. It wasn't as much as Shalesd and Cal but I was definitely grateful. She didn't have to do that, I was not her child. Whatever reason Aunt Tina left me something, I knew I would need it. I thought about getting my own apartment with it, but I also knew that eventually the money would run out. I didn't have a damn job to pay the bills so I second guessed that quick.

I wanted to be optimistic about Shalese and her dads relationship but I couldn't help to wonder was he only taking them for the money. Shalese still had about three and a half years before she was legally grown, and Cal..... shoot, need I say more! That baby was only eleven years old, he don't know anything about his fourty grand. Not to mention the social security checks that they'll get. Because Aunt Tina kept a job, that would be another great source of income monthly.

Four days later, It was the morning of Aunt Tina's funeral and I was more scared at that point than ever before. It could have been selfish of me but I wasn't scared about saying goodbye to Aunt Tina, I was afraid of what would happen to me. Shalese came in the room and gave me her cell phone and said, "Here call Dre. He called twice, tell dat nigga get you a phone!" She said jokingly. "I know right." I replied.

I called Dre back and he asked me if it was okay to come to support the family at Aunt Tina's funeral. I told him yes because we needed all the support possible. Not only was he a positive influence on Cal, he was also positively influencing me. I was a seventeen year old virgin. My first reaction to that statement was proud. That quickly wore off when I realized that there was nobody to love me or even thought after everything that happened she would give a care where I would end up. Nope, that was not the case at all.

Cal held up better than anyone expected him to at the funeral. Shalese on the other hand was still a mess, but by the time the repass came around she was much better. After it was all said and done Lese and Cal were gone. Though I still had the key to Aunt Tina's house I was really homeless. After the repass Dre and I hung around and chit chatted for a long while. I only told him a little about what was going on. There was no way in hell I wanted him to know the ugly raw truth. He sensed that I was full of crap right off the back though. "Stacie do you have plans for tomorrow?" "I don't think so, Oh....wait school if I make it!"

I do not get bus tickets because of the address I use, and Aunt Tina use to give me three dollars and fiffy cent for an all day fare. Sometimes she would get me a weekly pass because it was more convenient and it was cheaper." "Say no more! I will make sure you get back and fourth, but if you don't feel like school tomorrow take another day off." "Hear me out Stacie, that is not normal advice but under the circumstances, you might just need more time." "I was thinking about it." I replied. "Do you need a place to stay?" I tried to assure him I was fine. All the while I was screwed.

Coincidently he just so happen to be a man of many ventures and cell phones. He caught me side ways when he said, "Here take this." It appeared to be a brand new I80 touch screen. At first I played like I couldn't take the phone. When he insisted I hesitated no more! When I got out of Dre's car I dragged my feet to the house. Seemingly how scared I was, I did not know how I was going to make it through the night. Just as I closed the door behind me the cell phone rang scaring the cowboy shit out of me. "Hello." It was Dre. "Don't hesitate to call me if you need me. I think you're not telling me everything, I want you to know that I am here for you." "Okay I will." I hung up the phone. "Damn! He just don't know I need somebody right now."

The conversation we had was different, I could tell Shalese wasn't comfortable. But maybe it wasn't a bad thing having her dad there to intervene in her life more. It would be for the best. She asked me if I was going to be okay. I was turning into a great liar, because of course I said yes. I told her to keep in touch with me on that phone. She found that pretty amusing. The fact that Dre had given me the phone and I did not ask for it.

Once I got off of the phone with Shalese, I pulled out my diary and started writing. As I sat there in what use to be my Aunt Tina's home I became flustered. The more quieter it got the more and more mice came out. At that point suicide ran through my mind. I had no one to live for and I was becoming weary. I realized I could not stay in that house and have a promising future. After writing in my diary I was still not able to get comfortable and find sleep. I was so darn afraid to go back upstairs, but I needed to take a walk. Walking up the stairway felt like I was walking through the walls of a vacant house. It was so cold! Reluctantly I had a vivid imagination because imagining that things were normal helped me over come my fears in some ways.

I got some cash out of my stash spot and left out. Before I left the house I already had a clue where I was headed. I think I was a bit shocked myself. The first person I saw as I was leaving out of the door was Davon. "Oh Lord!" I thought to myself. How bad did my luck have to be before things would go right I wondered. I ignored the fact that I saw him and started on my way.

"Hey!..... Excuse me." I could not believe my ears and for some odd reason I was not afraid. I stopped dead in my tracks and faced him as he walked toward me. My face said it all, and scared wasn't it! "What's your name again?" I thought I had to be getting punked or was this some kind of joke. "I am Stacie!" "Stacie I'm sorry to hear about your aunt, was it?" "Yeah she was my aunt." "Shorty I know you don't have anything to do with the things your cousin get in to, fifteen years old. Her age speaks for itself." "Yeah you right, but I aint the first, man your cousin is a freak!" "Alright I'm done, what do you want?" "Bottom line is this, I gave her lil brother a few pills to sell and I want my money." "You did what?" "I wouldn't have never bothered shorty if that hoe sista of his aint steel my money!" Before I said anything I took a deep breath.

"How much is it that he owes you?" "Two hunned!" "Go figures." I mumbled. "Is there anyway you'll let me pay you back when I get the money. I am sorry for what Shalese did but I can't change it." "Alright shorty because you are so cool and I like how you get down for your fam, this one Imma let roll off, oh and you aint no punk either!" I gave him a fake smirk so I could hurry and be on my way. I let out a huge sigh of relief. He looked at me and shook his head before walking off.

No doubt, in the hood that is not how things normally roll. Maybe that was Aunt Tina who had my back. On my way to the store I wanted to call the only real person I could. Which was a shame being as though I just met him like a week ago. Mama's family was small but scattered and on my father side was a bunch of damn junkies and alkies. I wasn't a big socializer and that left me friendless. I had no one. I saw an older man outside of the store, he didn't look like a crack head but I could tell he could use a cold one.

"Excuse me sir can you get me a half paint of Smirnoff Vodka and a cranberry juice? I left my I.D home, you can get something if you like. "Sure I'll take a double deuce if you can." I gave him the money for my stuff and just gave him a five dollar bill for himself. Hmmm, I knew he was a beer drinker! It was a moment of humor for me. I have taken a drink once before and I promised I would not drink anymore but my circumstances left me dysfunctional in more than stoop. I brought me a pillow and a cup of ice out with me. Before I knew it I was tore the hell up! I mean white girl wasted! The street lights were glistening and I felt no pain. Ups there she go! At one point I thought I mastered the art of being horny. However it was more apparent that I didn't. It seemed like my hormones were becoming more enraged. I wasn't making it as a nun, that was out of the question. I pulled out the phone and contemplated calling Dre. I probably sat there twirling my phone in my hand for about thirty minutes. Time was not of the essence because school was out of the question for the next day.

Bzzzzz, Bzzzzzz, Bzzzzz. "What the heck is that? OMG, it's the darn phone! Yaaay it's Dre!" I immediately answered it. "Hello Coach." "What I tell you bout that Coach stuff." We laughed. "Well since you are a coach I thought I could take advantage of your skills and talents. "Say what!" Dre said. "You heard what I said, it would be appealing to me if you could teach me something. "You got me mind boggled Stacie, and what could that be?" "For clarification purposes, you don't have an old lady do you?" "Hahaha, you funny as hell, but naw I told you I didn't have one. The chick I was dating is a done deal." "Okay enough said!"

"So what is it that you want me to teach you?" "Sex!" "WHOA! Did you just say what I think you said?" "I'm quite sure I did!" "Stacie look, I know you're going through some things right now but don't make any decisions you'll regret in the long run." "So you're saying that if you screw me tonight, in the long run I'm gonna regret it!" "No No No...... that's not what I'm saying. I will never intentionally hurt you, you have been hurt enough." "And how would you know that!" "Well Stacie I still feel like you're not telling me everything." "Okay so what if I'm not, just come get me!" This time I said it with a demanding tone. I didn't know what I was getting myself into but I couldn't turn back then. At least that's what the alcohol said. The alcohol took me to higher heights.

boots to entice him a bit. Before heading back downstairs I cleaned my face up and freshened my vodka breath. I heard the horn blow and my heart dropped. When I looked out the window I notice his black volvo sitting there. I hurried downstairs with my over night bag. Carefully placing the key in the lock, my hands were trembling as I locked the door. I didn't want Dre to see that I was pissy drunk, he would of really thought I was talking out the side of my neck then. That fact was kind of hard to hide though!

My birthday was in five months and I would be eighteen, Dre on the other hand was twenty-six. At first the age difference thing had me freaked out, but I surely got over it. As I approached the car I heard the car doors unlock. When I got in the front seat all I could see was Dre's front teeth. I couldn't help but to laugh at him. Dre and I went to Silver Moone to grab a bite to eat and then we went to his apartment. I was grateful he did not recognize my drunkenness yet.

He pulled up to his apartment complex which was located in Cedonia. Compared to the projects, living in the Cedonia area was like living in the county. Cedonia was clean and very quiet, filled with home owners. Once we were inside we sat down and ate. The vodka was really about to make a statement so anything that was going to happen needed to hurry up. Dre had a one bedroom apartment that was truly designed for a man. There was no touch of a woman at all. I call myself going to the bathroom to clean my teeth, and my drunk behind took a dive. I just laid there. Obviously Dre heard me. He rushed in only to witness me on the floor grinning.

"Damn girl...... you drunk!" "That's right I am drunk, I didn't mean it though! I was just scared to be alone!" "Stacie, I asked you were you gonna be okay, you could of came here in the beginning." "I know Dre, I was suppose to go with my mother but I decided to wait for the weekend. This weekend the house is getting cleaned out and after that I'll be gone too." There was no way I was telling him the truth about my screwed up life!

need. I definitely didn't see the since in that. Enough about me it was time for me to see what's up with us! Dre helped me off of the floor and took my shoes off. Like a lifetime movie or something he carried me to the bed and laid my head on the pillow. By then the damn room was spinning. He gently slid my pants off and tucked me under the covers. It was about three minutes later when I noticed the place went pitch black. There were two candles lit on the mantle. I managed to peep and see Dre taking off his clothes. He got in the bed with a tank top on and a pair of Joe boxers. I thought he was going to jump on me like a hound. That wasn't the case at all, he laid beside me and placed his arm around me. He asked me was I okay then he ordered me to get some rest.

I turned my back toward his front and we cuddled. Everything was comfortable until I felt his hard manhood on my backside. Then it was on! I turned on my back and slid my panties off. He wasted no time following my lead and taking his underwear off too. Dre wasn't a small guy by far, I would guess he wore between 195 and 200 pounds easy. Those stats alone had a chick nervous. Dre went down under the sheets and caressed my clitoris with his tongue.

That was an amazing feeling of emotion that took over my body! And what the hell was I waiting for again! I moaned softly biting my bottom lip. When I rubbed his head I noticed that he had a good grain of hair. I had a lot of random thoughts running through my mind. Thereafter he finished introducing his tongue to my kitty cat, he licked and kissed his way up to my breast. As small as I was my breast had a nerve to be a size C cup already. Before I knew it the pleasure quickly turned to agonizing pain. Pain that I could not wait to end. He whispered in my ear, "Relax your body your in for a long ride." I did not pay that comment no mind! I was ready, at least I thought so once again! He sucked my neck softly then his penis entered my body. I gasped for air like someone was trying to suffocate me! It felt like it was my last breath recirculating.

kitty started loosening up but the pleasure had not returned yet. To make a painful story short, I didn't know how a woman could ever get use to this painful feeling. It was finally over and I was about to ball up in the fetal position. Dre kissed me on my cheek, then went to the bathroom and got both of us a warm rag. I thought that was so sweet of him. Hearing all of Shalese's stories none of them ended with washing up.

After wiping off, I fell straight to sleep in dream world. Dre sat at the bottom of the bed and played madden. In my sleep I could hear Dre's phone keep going off. Obviously he was rejecting it because it was ringing back to back. Later I heard him whispering telling whoever was on the phone that they better not come over. As tired and drunk as I was I could care less, and besides there were no strings attached between us. It gave me more motivation not to rush into anything with him though. I was young and some could even say I was dumb, but if I was a fool, I was going to be my own and no one else's. It was all to clear that there was someone else. Whether they broke it off or not she still had feelings.

Chapter Five

B ack to the bs!" I thought to myself! I insisted that Dre take me back to Aunt Tina's because I was so afraid of what would happen between Dre and I next. I always felt like I had to have mind power over a man so I would not get used. I left without breakfast and all. It was Wednesday, two days away from the weekend. Dre was a paramedic, that dude was off until Monday. Once I was at the house I saw that I was bleeding.

"What the hell!" I went off, I picked up the phone and called Shalese. "Hey Shalese!" "Hey cousin!" Shalese said all pumped. "Lese are you alone?" "No.... Why, are you okay?" "I do not know cuz! I did it last night!" "You did what last night?" "You know what I did, I had sex!" "WHAT?" "Oh my gracious are you for real!" "YES... Now shut up and listen! Lese why am I bleeding?" "Oh guuurrrrrl that is normal most people bleed after their first time." "Oh seriously!" "Yes, hun seriously!" You'll be okay." "Did it hurt like hell?" "heck yeah!" " What I don't get is, why do you still do it if it hurts like that ." "Girl please after a few times the pain turn into pleasure. Aww my big cousin calling me for advice, I feel honored!" Shalese said laughing.

"I did, but there is something else too. Last night Davon stopped me and what he told me blew my mind. You know that money you took." "Yeah." "He had Cal working it off and now since you and Cal are gone he came to me to see what's up." "Oh Stase I am sorry, when he come home please and tell him to call me." "I will, but Stase can you not tell him about what I did." "I wont!"

The conversation between Shalese and I ended as I heard my stomach talking. I should have ate something, I thought. At times I made the dumbest decisions. Dre gave me sixty dollars to get through the rest of the week. He told me to use that for school and my personals until he get paid next week. In a great sense, I wanted to call Dre and relieve all of my stress and just let him love me, but I was too afraid. For one, I could not stand the thought of rejection, but to think that the feelings I began to develope could actually put a strain on things. I ate a hot ham and cheese sandwhich and drunk a cold pepsi. There wasn't much to do this time of day, people were either at work or at school. I called Shalese back and asked her to meet me at barnes and nobles. But first my body was in need of a hot bath. I soaked the swelling down on my kitty cause that thang was thumping. Sore was an understatement.

I couldn't wait to see my cousin, I missed them being here already. When I looked out the window and saw Davon out front I changed directions and went out the back door. The weather had gotten brisk, so the fact that I had on a hat and scarf didn't look crazy. It was ideal to dress for the weather, but I almost think I over did it. I was covered up like a nun, trying to hide from the truth. The truth that I was no longer a virgin. A nice hot cup of chocolate would be so nice right now.

The bus ride was quiet but I never liked the bus. Barnes and Nobles or the library would always give me time to reflect and gain insight. Once inside, I ordered a cup of hot chocolate with mellows. Uh ohhh here comes big mouth! "Stacie, hey cuzin!" "Hey Shalese, babe what's up with the sweats?" "Stase my father is a dam hound, sniffing around and shit! All my tighties, he aint even having it! We argued my first night there! Anyway how are you?" "Besides cramping I am good." "What are you drinking?" "Cocoa." I replied." You should here before now. "Shalese asked me what was I going to do after this weekend. She was so worried. I told her I would be okay but she wasn't buying it. "Stacie do you want to come and live with us?"

"NO WAAY!.....I couldn't impose on your dad like that!" "Stacie it's not imposing, you are family. How about Dre?" "What about him?" "Well, can you go with him?" "Eeeew No! I can't have him thinking I need him already." "Stacie you shouldn't be so stubborn, you do actually need somebody!" "There are people who really love you like me." "Stacie you are like my oldest sister and I do not want anything to happen to you." A big ole crocadile tear came down my face. Ready to take Shalese up on her offer I quickly regained my strength and declined. I was tired of being a burden on other people.

For that quick moment I began to feel weak and scared. While Shalese and I sat there, Dre text the phone several times. Dre seemed to be a good guy but for so long all my heart knew was hurt and pain. I didn't think I would ever find happiness. However if I did, would I accept it. Could I be stupid, or I just don't want to be hurt anymore. The man who was suppose to love me the most despised and abandoned me. Shalese and I hung out for hours. Her dad told her to take the rest of the week off. Although Cal had the same option he went to school anyway. I could not wait to talk to him. I pictured me choking the life out of him but that image soon faded. I didn't want a good boy like Cal getting caught up in the streets. Where I was from the street would chew you up like a lion then when it's finish with you, it will spit you back out.

Finally Shalese and I said our goodbyes and went our separate ways. On the bus ride home I text Dre back. I lied and told him I was sleep when he text me. He asked me was I going to be okay alone. Yes was my response. I lied again! Dre didn't get off the phone until I agreed to stay the weekend with him. On the inside I was jumping for joy but that hard core outer body wouldn't let me give in. Seeing the life that Dre was making for himself inspired me to think more about quite appealing. Now that I know that is accomplished, it is time to take my brain to the next level. What is beauty without brain? I had Shalese to thank for the boost of confidence. On a bad day that girl was still upbeat.

My cramps were finally gone and my energy was restored. I was looking forward to school tomorrow. When I got home I washed my hair and put a mushroom wrap in my hair. I got the idea from Keri Hilson. I loved her. For that hair style I didn't need any tracks, my hair was a pretty good length. I always took pride in my hair. That was the one thing I didn't want to change. I showered and laid my clothes out before I snuggled myself on the couch. Laying there Dre and I getting it on was the vision in my head. I grabbed the phone and called him. He answered sounding tired. "I'm sorry did I wake you?" "You good, is...." I cut him off. "Yes everything is okay and I am not drunk, I just wanted to say goodnight. Oh and I would like to thank you again for all that you have done for me.

"Awww aint that sweet!" Dre replied. "It would be a better night if you were here." "Do you mean that Dre?" "Hell yeah, I do!" "Well I will be there this weekend." "Okay I can live with that, you going to school right!" "Yes Sir." "Get some sleep and call me in the morning." "Okay night night." I replied.

I only had two days left to figure something out. Reflecting back to what Shalese said, would have been enough to say problem solved. I guess for the average teen whose life wasn't so shaky. Dre threw out a few suggestions too, but they all involved me staying at his place. I didn't know if his offer was extended to me as a permanent situation or not. Even if it was I was too young for that type of living arrangement. By the time I turn twenty I would be more experienced than a thirty year old. Let alone looking at the facts, most teen relationships do not last forever anyway. All I wanted was a normal teenage life for a change.

Friday, Shalese told me Saturday. I was freaking out. Since Shalese's dad didn't know I was still staying there I stayed out of his sight. If I knew they were coming a day earlier I would have taken my bags and prepared a little better. Once they were finished I took my time and walked around the block. As I walked up on the door I noticed a big gray pad lock on the door. I reached the door and at that moment I felt like a helpless child. All I could do was stand there and cry. All of my things were in there. I didn't know if they threw my stuff away or took it thinking it was Shalese's.

I didn't bother to take my key out and embarrass myself. There was no way around the pad lock. I wasn't normally a crier but the older I got the more things seemed to stank. I did not know what to do. Not only was I embarrassed as all hell, but I was mad and very confused. So many evil thoughts ran across my mind. I couldn't decide whether to call Shalese or Dre but I wasn't sleeping on nobody's streets. Those two were all I had and now I was forced to choose. I knelt down in the stooping position and put my head on my knees and cried like a baby, I did not care who was watching. "God why are you doing this to me, I am your child. Why do you hate Meeeeee?"

I felt a strong hand palm my shoulder and my fear grew greater. I thought I was about to meet my maker. I sat there for about fifteen seconds longer with my head down. I was too afraid to lift my head up and see who was touching me. "It is going to be okay shorty!" The voice said. A slight smile came upon my face because it was a familiar voice. Me and the voice didn't have a great track record but it showed that he wasn't a superb son of a you know what!

"C'mon get up shorty. Look don't worry about getting me back the money, do you want me to break this off for you?" When I looked up, I saw the concern on Davon's face, and I gave in. He wiped my tears away and put his arms around me. He took me around back because there were a few nosy folks out front. "Be honest with me

I don't have anything right now, and I don't have anywhere to go!" "Dam foreal! Where did Shalese and Calvin go?" "They moved with their dad." "Oh, he wouldn't let you come there?" "He probly would have but I didn't ask." I went on and told Davon a little bit about me and why staying with Shalese or Dre was a dead last resort. To my surprise he understood. Then brilliantly he came up with a thirty day solution, or should I say scheme.

Davon was familiar with the ways of the projects. Normally when someone moved out the maintenance men would come during that same week. However, if the tenant passed away they would give the family between 30 and 45 days to clean it out. Davon and his home boy Rod paid this guy to cut the lock off. He said it would be best if I used the back door only. I was appreciative to Davon but I wondered was he doing this for a price. Although he said the money was no longer an issue, I still was skeptical about his reasoning. I told Davon that I had plans the weekend so I wouldn't be there and I would be back on Sunday. He was cool with that and he agreed to watch the house for me. I in turn gave him my cell number in case he needed to contact me for any reason. After the chain of events that went on that day I still found a happy bone to share with Dre. I couldn't wait until he came and got me.

When I packed my things, I packed more than usual because I knew eventually Dre would be my temporary solution. I text Dre and told him I was ready and to pick me up on the side street. He text me back and said okay. When Dre text back and said he would be there in ten minutes, I gave myself a ten minute makeover. Mind you Davon was still there.

"Aright Davon thank you so much for everything, I am about to bounce see you on Sunday." "Aight shorty, Dammm....you look good!" "Aight boy see ya!" I dashed out the back door to Dre's car.

that had me wanting to feel the pain again. The pain of his penis thrusting my puddin bowl.

"How was your day sweet lady?" "Wow, don't even ask about it!" "It was that bad?" "You know what Dre, now that I am with you, I'm all good." "Aww go head girl you don't like me like dat!" Dre joked. "More than you could imagine." "Dre can I be honest with you?" "That's how I like it, wussup with you?" "I would love to stay with you, I just need to grasp the idea of something good really going on in my life. There is never anything good ever happening to me and I can't stand the thought of what we have going wrong. All because we moved to fast. As quick as relationships happen, I have seen them end just as fast." Dre was floored. "Dag I thought you were trying to be a pimp or something, but what you said actually makes since. Just know that the offer still stands."

"But naw, all jokes aside I hear you, but Stacie please know that I'm here for you." "Thank you and I do know." We pulled up to Dre's apartment and by the look of things he went an extra mile to entertain me. I could see the red light shining through the curtains from his window. When Dre noticed the expression on my face He smiled so hard. He ran over to me and swept me off of my feet. All my bags fell and I was truly in happy mode. We looked into each others eyes and something magical happened. He seemed to be able to see my hurt through my joyful moments. The same thing occurred when I looked deep into his eyes. His eyes told me a story. He picked up my bags and we headed to the building. Walking up the last stair case before his apartment, I smelled the aroma of honey suckle and vanilla.

I was in awe when Dre opened the door. In the entry way were twenty dollar bills leading to the bed. I looked over at the table and saw the candles burning. Surrounded by a bowl of strawberries. Dre ended up walking around me because I hadn't picked my mouth up off the floor yet. The lamp had a soft red bulb in, which it set

I finally made my way in and took off my coat.

Before I could sit down, Dre came over to me and whispered in my ear let the real coaching begin. I tilted my chin up and giggled. What was a girl to do. I wanted to just tell him everything, stay there and never go back. I imagined the night being just about sex but to my surprise it wasn't. Dre and I talked, laughed and drunk some wine together. Well, I drunk the wine and he drunk the goose. He asked me can I dance and of course I said yes. Even if I couldn't, I wasn't gonna tell him that. He would have had to figure it out on his own. Dre got up went to the radio and put on Ace Hood, body to body. Now that was more like it. My eyes squinted awkwardly before Dre said, show me what you got. Being young and naive I told him there was no way I could dance to that slow song. Then a light bulb came on in my head. "Ohhhhhh I see!"

I slowly stood to my feet and it was as if I had been dancing for years. I worked that thang like a pro! He stood up and picked up each twenty from the floor. He put them on my body anywhere he could. I pushed him on the chair and gave him a lap dance. Once again the alcohol had done did it again. I was impressed by my darn self! Far as Dre, he loved it. Instead of my come get me boots I had on my multi color stilettos. Along with my straight legs and a multicolor sequined halter top.

My wrap was the cutest and my confidence was skies the limit. Dre stood back up and kissed me speechless. The night was young, neither one of us was good at cooking. Eventually one of us had to learn something because hot pockets were only okay sometimes. I was so hungry that the hot pockets at that moment tasted like home made lasagna. I took the initiative to run us a hot bubble bath. The water was near scorching but yet spine tingling. The bath was just intended for us to freshen up. By the time we got out Dre's manhood was extremely stiff. I was in for it then, I thought to myself. What Dre didn't know was, I prepared myself mentally to go hard and take it like a champ, as well as throw it back!

and that was something I admired. Being with him made me feel older, much older actually. Dre picked me up and carried me to the bed. This time on the night stand sat some body oil and massaging gel. He laid me down and oiled my body while it was still a bit wet. It was so relaxing I took it all in. Not expectantly, I got up and signaled him to lay down on the bed. He smirked but he did it anyway. I took his smirk as him trying to call me out. I was fitting to show his butt! I flipped the script and body oiled every nook, cranny, and inch of his body, From his head to his toes. Once I was in the midsection I fondled his penis. Then I held the messaging gel above it and poured some on. Before I knew it I went to work!

I rubbed and massaged it intensively. He closed his eyes and bit his bottom lip. That was all I needed to see. The ultimate sign of approval! I began to explore and taste the raw intimacy, and I could feel him lift his head up to watch me. Followed by him sighing and falling back down. I showed up and showed out. When he pushed me off of him and flipped me over I didn't know what to think. He proceeded to spread my legs and then every inch of him penetrated me. Was I not doing it good or what! Shockingly this time it was pleasing. I let out a huge sigh and pulled him closer to me. I didn't know what an orgasm felt like quite yet so I didn't have a clue what to expect. Anyway, we went at it for about 20 long minutes before Dre's little soldiers came marching. Within those 20 minutes Dre's coaching taught me a few things. I was a tad bit sore but it wasn't anything I couldn't handle. Dre and I cuddled and shared a few fantasy details. Right then I wanted to tell him all of my troubles.

"Stacie are you coming to the game with me tomorrow?" "Sure!" I replied. "Cal haven't been to any practices this week, do you think he will still play this season?" "Dre that is a good question. I need to speak to him though because he has been interacting in some things that aint no good for him." "Yeah, like what if you don't mind me asking." "Well he got caught up in a little drug drama with the guys in the court across from us."

huh!" "Yes and it's over, I promise you!" "Okay Stacie if you say so!" By the projection in his voice I could tell he was mad. We conversed for a little while longer and then we were both fast to sleep. I planned on taking only two of the twenties instead of the whole stack. I knew Dre was just looking out for me but I didn't want him to feel like he had to give me money every time we were together, and I darn sure didn't want to feel like a prostitute. I was hoping for a relationship to build; Dre would be my hero and take me away.

The rest of the weekend Dre and I had such a good time. We did everything from laugh, sex, try cooking, went to the movies, and a bunch of other exciting things. That was the best weekend my young life had ever had! Dre and I did not want the weekend to end. He struck me as the sensitive type. Not overly sensitive but sensitive enough to get his feelings involved. Far as I could tell he wasn't lacking much so why his last girlfriend left him, was beside me. I asked him about the night I heard him telling some chick not to come over. He explained to me that it was his ex girlfriend. In her head it was okay for her to still pop up when she wanted too. I believed him because he had no good reason to lie.

Chapter Six

The rendezvous Dre and I had was over and I had to return to the hell hole. I used the back door like Davon told me too. Before I entered I could hear music coming from inside. Davon agreed to watch the place but not stay here I thought. When I walked in the door I wanted to tum around and walk right back out! Bad enough I had Dre on my back asking me why he dropped me off here and not my moms. Still lying to him, I said that I was moving in with her after the house was cleaned out. Originally I had told him something different and that sucker did not forget a word

To walk up in there and see Davon and two other guys up in there made me sick to my stomach. They were sitting at a broke down looking table on some dag on milk crates. Them being their didn't bother me that much but the fact that they were bagging crack was unacceptable. I stood there looking like a crazy fool. The way I felt inside was devastating. There was no way in hell I was going to live like this. He gave me know choice, I had to leave. I told myself two more weeks of this madness and I would bounce. I was trying to wait on the ten grand Aunt Tina had left me. Then I would at least have a starting point. But right now I have nothing. Dre, he really seems like a nice guy, but what if it don't work! I would be right back at square one. I was so lost, I didn't know what to do.

Shalese and her dad was at each others throat all the time so that definitely was not an option. If only I could hold on a couple more called survival. This wasn't the person I wanted to become, but hey what the hell it was what it was!

When I was a little girl I pictured myself being a nurse. It was back to business for me. On Monday I carried my behind right back to school and my Dre was back at work. For us seeing each other, I predicted it to be a dry week because he had to do a straight seven. Everyday I came home and went upstairs and did my homework. Once I was done I wrote in my diary The only thing kept me going was the anticipation of seeing Dre again and the ten grand I had coming. I laid there and cried myself to sleep most nights. My nights were lonely and my heart was filled with grief. The floor was so cold and hard that at my young age my bones and back started to ache daily. I am guessing Davon felt the tension between us because he came and approached me on Wednesday.

"Stacie I am not trying to take over or anything......but I was thinking if you help me I will help you. And by that, I mean I will make sure you are good. I promise." Davon said. "Davon it's not you, but I do not like all those guys in and out of here!" "Okay I understand, I will deal with it today. The last thing I want Stacie is to make you more uncomfortable. I am so sorry."

"Shorty you are really cool and I want to help you. If you don't like it and you want it to stop then it stops today." "Alright thanks Davon." I replied. All the furniture had been taken when they moved everything out. So all that left me with was the floor and the blanket. I took off my clothes at night to make a pillow, but the nights that it was too cold I had to leave my clothes on. I wanted so badly to just say the hell with it and go stay with Dre, but the thought that he would eventually abandon me too kept lurking. My heart was so filled with pain and my family life was nonexistent. At that point I really yearned for my mother. I picked up my phone and called her. She picked up and I just cried.

that she sounded sober. But then I thought about it, if she was sober why didn't she come back for me. Knowing that Aunt Tina wasn't here anymore! "Mama what am I going to do, I don't have no where to goooo!" I could barely get my words out over my crying and sniffling. Mama actually started crying! Then the phone fell quiet. "Mama are you still there?" I cried out. "Yes baby I hear you." That was the sincerest I heard mama in a long time. I think she might of been a little choked up too. "Stacie I am sorry but Mama is not in a place to do anything. I'm sorry I did this to you Stacie. I love you Stacie but........." "But what mama you fucked up my life and now you can't even help me fix it! I did not ask to be here ya know! Why did I even bother?"

"Stacie I'm staying at a friends house, his name is Mr. Ronald I don't think he'll mind if you come and stay over here. For a moment I felt like a kid in the candy store. Until she said you can stay here until I get out of rehab if you want too. I leave for rehab next week. Then my thoughts were hell no, she just trying to pond me off again. What if his ass die too then I'm back to square one. I hate square one, it's time for part two in my life. I hung up with Mama with nothing accomplished.

I texted Dre and told him good night and stay safe, then I took my miserable self to bed. The next morning when I woke up I had bags under my eyes. I cried so much the night before, I looked like a powder puff girl. As time went on, Davon and I became real cool. I mean cooler than I could have ever imagined. He came from a screwed up situation himself. His mother was a single mother of six children. She made her living by working in the super market. It was until one day she came home to find her house in flames. The sad part was, Davon's four brothers and sisters were inside and they burned to death. He told me how his mom couldn't afford a baby sitter so she often left his nine year old sister to watch the kids. The kids under her were seven, four, and, three. Davon had summer school that summer and his oldest brother was locked up. Davon's but to go to jail sent her crazy.

Davon had no choice but to go with his dad. Who didn't have much of anything and didn't go the extra mile to try to get it either. Now he was out here trying to survive pretty much, like me. Looking at him, it was so hard for me to believe he was only twenty. His look ultimately told his life's story. He wasn't an ugly dude, but rough was a better description. The relationship between us was like a brother sister relationship. More than anything, I wanted to run away but then at the same time I felt guilty leaving him behind. I know I could of walked away if I wanted to, but he could of walked away from me too but he didn't. Davon couldn't stand the fact of me having to fend for myself so if I needed it he would get it. He was not the same Davon I saw choking the life out of Shalese's tail. He treated me with mad respect. I could not believe how comfortable I became there with Davon. He was like a brother I never had. He told me I should go be with dude though, because that was no way for me to live. I told him I needed a little more time to see if Dre and I could really be together before I made a move like that.

After that conversation he went out and broke his neck to get me a blow up mattress. It wasn't a tough task because he did not have the money, but he had to go to like three or four stores to find a good one. Before I agreed to let Davon stay there, he stayed over at the Duke motel on Pulaski Highway. What a waist I thought! I told him he might as well come and stay with me until our time was up. The check had not come yet from Aunt Tina so I started to get worried. It was already close to thirty days. It was time for me to finally make up my mind.

It was time for me to talk to Dre about me coming to stay with him. However, the thirty days had came and gone and no one showed up to do anything to the house. I figured we might as well just stay here until the end. Whatever the hell that meant. I didn't understand the odd connection between Davon and I. We never had sex nor did became more strain. I wasn't mad because he was picking up a lot of work. Because he worked so much we probably saw one another once a week. Dre didn't like it and he insisted that I moved in. What he didn't know was I now wanted that too. But was that the right decision? I questioned. Don't get me wrong, Dre was the ultimate catch. But sometimes I couldn't decide what type of panties I should wear let alone how to be a live in girlfriend. So yes, the thought of me being obligated to someone who was perfect in my eyes terrified the hell out of me. Since Dre worked a lot, Davon and I hung out together on most Fridays. I soo looked forward to hanging with him most nights, he always made me laugh. On the Fridays I would stay home Davon would give me money to order Chinese. Then we would grub out. A few of us would sit around, drink, play cards, and talk about the inevitable. Davon was a real freak. A lot of the project chicks was on him, and I mean heavy too.

I wouldn't say he had to pay for sex, but from what I could see he paid way more than he weighed. I'm not sure what that was about but he was very generous with his money. I began to think a lot about Dre, so I decided to call him.

"Hey bay I'm on a call, let me call you back!" Dre said. "Okaaaay!" I mumbled. That was a little suspect, because even when Dre was already at a scene he had more words to say than that. Oh well I didn't think too much of it. I was so darn hungry my naval was touching my spine. I couldn't wait til tonight for Chinese. A ham and cheese sandwich with some plain chips on honey wheat would do for now. Lately my appetite had increased enormously. I was never a big eater but these days I went back for seconds and thirds. Davon came in with this dude I really wasn't feeling. I couldn't put my finger on it but he looked sneaky. When I spoke to him he just nodded his head like he was the god father or somebody. "Wack ass!" I said to myself.

"Hey girl!" Davon said all eager. "Hey Day what's good?" "You!" He replied. "Are you staying home tonight or are you going with ole about an hour or two then we can make the order." "You good til I get back Stacie?" "Yeah I'm straight, but hurry back." "Alright see you when I get back." Wow..........Davon really look nice today. That guy had a fresh cut and shape up. Finally he trimmed off all that darn wool off his face, looking like wolfy!

From head to toe his clothes made a statement. When Davon left I called Shalese to see what has been going on with her and Cal. Shalese was still up to her same old tricks. Calvin was a totally different story. Shalese said that her dad and stepmother decided to send him away to boarding school. It was more than one occasion that they found drugs in his backpack. My first thoughts were, What a coward of a father. But then after thinking about the situation maybe he did the only thing he knew how. I just hoped he didn't take my little cousins for the money. Before we hung up Shalese did give me some good news. She said that Aunt Tina's policy was mailed off so we should have our money soon.

I showered and got ready for an all nighter. That night Davon and I had a ball. He invited a few homeboys over and I even invited the girl Tionna from next door. That chick was wild but funny as hell. We got white girl wasted and put on a show. Tionna sat on Davon's lap and I instantly cut him the evil eye. Without hesitating he got up laughing and excused himself to the bathroom. I tried not to make it obvious but I was jealous. I pranced my drunk tale to invade his privacy in the bathroom. His face spoke a thousand words when I busted in on him. Davon knew I was tore up so he kept right on about his business. Plus he was still on that brother sister bull shit. After what I saw, I couldn't say I still felt the same. I closed the door behind me and stood there licking my lips.

"Stacie what are you doing guurl?" "Oh boy please! Don't play with me Davon!" Davon tried to hurry up and zipping his pants and I jerked his body around and slid my tongue in his mouth. His first reaction was stand off mode. He didn't push me off but the fool

"What about ole boy Stacie?" "Dam Davon you'll mess up a wet dream." "I'll deal with that later." "Alright, I don't want no mess guurl!" Before I knew it that dude had his buddy in his hand. I slid down my jeans to my knees and bent over the sink. Right away penetrated me and I was literally sick to my stomach. His man piece was so darn big, it felt like I was constipated. For some awful reason he knew exactly how to do me. I normally moaned and groaned to the top of my lungs but we had company. I didn't want any of those nosy asses to know my business. Not yet anyway plus I was still seeing Dre.

When Davon and I were done, we looked goofy and sat there smiling at each other. Like a true thug he kissed my lips one more time, pulled up his pants and went right back downstairs. I sat on the toilet top puzzled with the crap face. I could not believe I done that nasty mess. Dre could never find out, I said to myself. Maybe there is a little slut in all of us, I thought. For a quick second I thought about Shalese and I laughed.

Far as Dre and I go, what he don't know won't hurt him. I sort of felt bad though, because Dre was a good dude. At the same time, here lately he has been acting kind of shady. He still paid my phone bill every month and gave me money whenever he saw me. Now that Davon and I have been shacking up he has been lacing me too. My clothes game stepped up a few notches and so did my self-esteem. Over the few weeks that past Davon and I began a sexual relationship. That was only due to Dre floating away. At first I thought it was my fault and maybe working a lot had something to do with it. But then I became accustomed to his schedule and I learned it like the back of my hand. Tionna and I became cool as hell too. I thought she was stuck up at first but when I got to know her, she was real down to earth.

After the night that Davon and I had sex our relationship picked up the pace to a fast start. After the night in question, I found out page. The relationship that Dre and I once had became more textual than sexual. Meanwhile I became Davon's Bonnie and he was my Clide. It wasn't until I caught Dre in a lie and found out that he had been messing back with his ex girlfriend. I cut that escapade off completely. I am glad I didn't move in with that buster. But then this fool had the audacity to blame it on me. He said I allowed her back

Had I just came and stayed with him there would have been no time and space for her. Did he really say that! That was truly the lamest bull I had ever heard. He caught my favorite line before I cut his behind off. "What the hell eva!" I could of been laying up in there and he still would of screwed her again. It was something that wasn't over between them two, and he tried to replace her with me. Not on my watch! I already had a lot going on in my life as it was. Davon was my boo for real. The ten grand Aunt Tina left me finally came through. Me and Davon went and got an apartment on the south side of town. All the damn money went to furniture. Our bedroom set was a king size Ashley set from Value city. We bought two plasma flat screens. One was in the bedroom and one was in the living room. I didn't want a lot of furniture so the living room had a couch with leather pillows and a coffee table. Our dinning room had a table and chair set with a few pictures on the wall. That was it far as our furniture.

I considered myself completely moved on from Dre but this dude paid my cell every month. Eventually he would be back in touch I figured. Honestly I couldn't wait for that day because I wanted an explanation, but I wasn't pressed to ask for it. That one he gave me before came out of the old cracker jack box. Through all that I had going on I kept my behind in school. Weeks had gone by and I couldn't help but notice that my butt and hips had gotten bigger. I been recognized the increase in my appetite a month ago but then my clothes size was showing for it.

butt was knocked up! After we got our place, our furniture and a few pieces of clothes we invested in some work. For those who do not know, we bought some coke. I would cook it, bag it, and price all packages. Davon was the distributer. Which made since, he didn't dare want me on the front line.

Eventually our empire got big enough that we only sold weight. The transition happened over the course of three months. Things started to get hectic far as friendships go. Dudes were straight hating. Davon didn't want to see it though. On an average day I would go to school and Day would go down the jects and rock off the work. Tionna was already out of school so she was Davon's right hand when I wasn't around. Her and the dude Kalief kicked it every then and again, nothing serious. Kalief was the guy with the sneaky eyes. For the life of me I couldn't shake the feeling of not liking nor trusting him! But what could I say, he was Davon's boy. Kalief was still nickel and diming and always needed Day to bail him out of everything. I sensed a bit of jealousy if you ask me! Sometimes guys are so hard headed, they don't see things for what it really is. So ultimately like an ass, I had to play along until the mess hit the fan. Believe me when I say, it will hit the fan......! I guess you can say it's a gut feeling, maybe even a women's intuition.

Chapter Seven

t was February and the weather was blizzard like. My birthday was the sixth of February but I rarely celebrated it. Coincidently Davon's was on the eight of February. We made a pat to celebrate our birthdays together and enjoy them from then on. Normally I would go to Tionna's house after school and help Day with the sales, then we would go home around nine.

For some time I have been talking to my mother and she was doing well in her rehab program. I was proud of her effort. Mama wasn't stupid either, she knew exactly how Day and I made a living. That didn't bother her but for several reasons it bothered me though. For mama sake I would not bring her to my house just yet because work was always in session. Tempting her was the last thing I wanted to do. I loved looking in mama's eyes, they were beautiful. Her skin color was coming back nicely. She also started picking back up her weight and she took a trip to the dental school to get her some dentures. The program was a live in situation so Davon would pick her up on the weekends. Her and I would hang out and I would hook her hair up to build her lacking confidence. I was deeply trying to forgive her but it wasn't easy at all.

She was doing so good. I told her that as long as she promised to stay clean then she could come stay with us if she needed to. She loved to hear that. I told mama I might be pregnant and that I was scared. Like any sane mother, she told me everything was going to to me like glue was, "Stacie if you are pregnant please do not make the same mistakes I made!" Mama wanted me to finish school and get my education. She said depending on a man was the last thing I should do, which I kind of already knew. She made sure she voiced her opinion about me and Davon's choice of work. I knew that if I was pregnant the drugs had to be alleviated.

Me and mama actually had real parent, child talk, it brought tears to my eyes. I felt like she was almost back fully. I never had my mama sober and in my corner since I was about seven. That was a long time ago. When I mentioned the possibility to Davon he brushed the thought off. Then his ghetto tail came back and said, "Yup you might be cause dat booty getting mad phat!" By then my size eight jeans could not button anymore. I was pregnant but I was so far in denial. I just couldn't face it. I told mama a lot on our phone conversation but I didn't tell her that I was afraid the baby could be Dre's. Davon was an obvious possibility but she knew nothing about Dre. I made the doctors appointment after my birthday so I could still party without feeling guilty. My intentions weren't to get pissy drunk but I did plan to drink a few glasses of wine.

Shalese and I haven't seen each other in a while, and we barely talked over the phone anymore. It made me sick because it had much to do with her dad. I would call her phone sometimes and he would have it. Dude was on cock block time for real. I wanted so bad for her to come and celebrate my birthday with me, but I regretted to tell her about Davon and I. When I asked Davon what he thought about it. He basically said that I could tell her anything I wanted to but he did not want to be in her company. I mean don't get me wrong, I could respect that but........she is still my cousin.

For the mean time I decided to keep quiet. For once in my life I was happy. It was not the normal life for a seventeen year old but I was then in the drivers seat. The choices were all mine. I think that is why I could forgive mama so easily. For once, what she did to me was pulling through her addiction. It felt so good having that lady around to help me plan the birthday party for me and Day. Thanks to Tionna and Davon, I now have a social circle. It wasn't big but it was more than I had at first. Tionna knew everybody. Of course Davon did too, living the street life. My birthday fell on a Friday which made Davon's that Sunday. The party was going to be on that Saturday to compliment both of our birthdays.

That Friday me, Tionna and mama got together so I could share my vision of the party with them. They thought I was good and crazy after I told them. I was literally the laugh of their day. One of me and Davon's common interest was a shapely woman. I wasn't a lesbian or anything but I loved a female with a nice figure. A banging body sent chills down my spine. I could definitely understand a mans attraction to a woman. A nice set of legs, a banging booty and last but not least a tight abdomen. A big cake wasn't enough I added a tempting dancer to the package. She was fitting to be the after party though. Just a little something to blow Davon's mind. I could picture me being blown away too. Most of the times before him and I had sex one of us would pop on a flick. The sex was like some ruff ryder shit, like DMX in belly. Crazy, Sexy, Good! Yes sex was a major common interest but we also had a passion for football too. So my imagination ran a little wild with the cheerleader and football story.

"We like tricks too.........she'll have to do mad tricks." Mama and Tionna died laughing, I cracked my own self up with that one. Our apartment was to small to accommodate our guess so we booked the party room at the Sheraton North. The space was good for about 100 people, we only invited about 50. After we booked everything we went to the mall. Mama had spiff taste. I almost thought Shalese and I were switched at birth. Shalese darn sure could dress, and looking at mama you could tell they had the same DNA. As Madea would say, they had the same Dana!

I did not get none of that good dressing DNA. My sense of style wasn't that sharp. I lived in a more black and white error of style a yellow shirt or dress. But I have to say it always looked good. After all the running around with the ladies I was beat. I wanted mama to stay the night but her program wasn't having that. Her curfew was at nine o'clock on Fridays and seven during the week. She had another three months which wasn't that bad. Tionna went her way and I took my tired behind home.

Davon was like a big kid, he kept calling and texting me. "What's up shorty? Happy birthday babe!" All that kind of mess! I was tickled pink because it was thoughtful. I text him back and asked him when was he coming home. Day text back and said give him about another hour and he would be there. That's all he ever needed was an hour! That night was one of those nights that I just wanted to be comfortable. A wife beater and a pair of boy shorts is what it was. I said to myself. After I showered I was able to adore my body in awe like I never did before, it was stunning. My belly had a round bulge shape and there was a dark line coming down the middle of it. At that moment there was no doubt in my mind that I was really carrying a baby in there. My hormones had kicked in over drive and I was horny all the time.

I had to check out my body once more. I stood in front of the mirror and lifted my wife beater, then rubbed my stomach in a circular motion. In my own little world, I never even noticed Davon coming in. He caught me rubbing my belly and picked me up and swung me around. "We having a baby for real!" "I think so!" I said joyfully. When he put me down he stood there starring at me like he was in disbelief. He then said, "Go in the room because I got Kalief in the living room. My face frowned. "I thought tonight we were gonna chill........alone!" "Chillax shorty he is not staying, I need to count out some stuff for him." "Oh aright! Day I want some pizza and lemonade from the carryout. Before you do what you do, can you get me something to eat." "Imma place the order over the phone and then run and pick it up." "Aright. "

Chapter Seven

I couldn't stand the thought of Kalief being in my house. It was something about his eyes! After ten minutes or so Davon came in the room and told me he will be back he was going to pick up the food. Then he had the audacity to ask me can Kalief stay in the living room and finish up. "Hell No! Are you serious?" I walked away from his tail! "Aight, Aight." Davon said. He swiftly ran out the room and I heard him telling Kalief to walk him to the store. I don't think Kalief liked me too much either because him and Davon use to be together 24-7. They both slept in motel rooms and had no regards to a normal life.

It was like Davon and I rescued each other from disaster. Not to mention all of the stories Davon had told me about Kalief. He was trigger happy and hotheaded. Davon came back in with my food and I was ready to smash. I did not eat in the bedroom because I was a messy eater. I slipped on my sweats and went to the dinning room. "Save me some pizza babe." "I know you and my lil man probly hungry but save daddy a slice!" My facial expression just went completely cold. Meanwhile Kalief's face did a three sixty as well. I call myself giggling it off but there was no true expression I could of made that would have told my adequate feelings. I tell you what, if looks could kill, somebody would have been dead. Then Kalief gave me a nod. The bastard never opened his mouth and guess what neither did I! I nodded my head right back! Please, why should I waist my darn breath on his scum behind. I knew he was scum I just wish I could prove it. Him and Tionna wasn't an item but he somehow managed to brainwash her too. I initially kept my ill feelings about him to myself. Besides the little bit I shared with Davon.

That night was the first Friday that Day and I not only turned in early, but we spent it alone. The drug life could be pretty tiresome. We talked a lot about the what ifs. Then we talked about Davon going back to school so that we could both do right and make an honest living. If I was knocked up we had to change for the baby's sake if nothing else.

my baby's piece of mind or well being. As much thug as Davon had in him I was afraid that all his talk about doing right was just talk. The streets was all Day knew. He been hustling since he was twelve to help his mama raise his brothers and sisters. Our past had a whole lot to do with the tight bond we built. The past was something Dre and I didn't have in common. Me and Day had so much in common it became natural being with him. I didn't have to try so hard.

Before I doze off the clock said eleven forty six. For me it was a little early, I was a twelve thirty person, even on school nights. The next morning Davon and I hit the jects to do our thing. He stayed outside across the court and I was in Tionna's house with the work. I still had so much to do for the party. I had to pick up the cake, and get Davon a gift. I needed to get mama so she could finish up the food for me. Unfortunately I wasn't able to get mama until late, because on Saturdays she took her G.E.D classes. I asked Diane to have the cake ready for pickup at twelve noon. So first thing was first, I decided to go get Davon's gift since it was only ten thirty. I already knew exactly what and where I was getting his gift from. Church square was a shopping center in walking distance from the projects. I became a regular customer in the downtown locker room up there.

Tionna and I walked up there and I grabbed a G-shot watch and a pair of the new Labron James for Davon. By the time we finished up there it was time for me to pick up the cake. At that point I was having a personal moment. I sort of wanted to be by myself. After we had picked up the cake we took a sedan back to her place. I gave Day the work, stayed in the sedan and I went on my way. From what I could see Tionna was mad cool but I really have not known her that long to say I trust her with my life at that time. She never showed any wicked intentions, I just was confident with the choice not to tell her everything.

I headed over to the Sheraton to get a head start on the decorating. It was one o'clock so I still made good time. After I decorated, I be leaving around four from her class. When I asked if she needed Davon to pick her up she insisted she was fine. I wasn't feeling that gesture. Mama was doing so well and the thought of her messing up sickened me. The time I had in between I planned to use it wisely. I went home and took a nap for about an hour. When I got up it was four thirty. I jumped up like I was running, late for something. Can you say pissed.com! I gave my own darn self a headache. Mama left me a message about twenty minutes earlier saying she was on her way. I also had a missed call from Davon.

The missed call from the other number was a shocker! It was Dre! I called Davon back first. He was always so loud over the phone, if I wasn't woke yet I was woke then. He sounded like he was in a noisy tunnel. "Hey suga!" "Hey babe!" I said matching his enthusiasm. "Wow I'm suga today huh!" "Girl stop the madness you know aint nothing or no one sweeter than you!" "Oh yeah, you probly told them other hoes the same thing, didn't you!" He smacked his lips and said you would mess up a wet dream if I starred in one. We both laughed. "Why didn't you answer the phone?" "Duh....cause I was sleep Davon!" "Dam Stacie don't bite my head off!" "Okay I'm sorry." I replied. "Davon what time will you be there tonight?" "We're not going together?" Davon asked. "NO WAY! I want it to be like its a first date or something. No boo I will meet you there." The tone in his voice let me know he really wasn't okay with that arrangement. He's a big boy he could handle it!

Calling Dre back was the last thing on my mind. At times I did regret me not putting my best foot forward as far as me and Dre's relationship went. He definitely was a good catch with a good head on his shoulder. What Davon and I shared was amazon but the foundation was rocky. Dre had already had a great career and much opportunity to move up in rank. The fact that he was not patient with me gave me the push to move on and forget about him. As I washed my hair it hit me that I was really pregnant and didn't know who my baby's father was.

hole and saw mama. I swung the door open, pulled her in and gave her a big bear hug. "Hey baby are you okay?" Mama said. "I don't know ma!" Then out of no where I began to cry. Ma looked at me with fear in her eyes. I could tell she didn't know what to do. Then suddenly her mothers instincts kicked in. She grabbed me and rubbed my wet hair. She was hell bent on everything being okay. "But Mama you don't understand!" I said sobbing all over the place. "Well then Stacie you need to help me understand. What is going on with you baby?" I ejected myself away from mama and pulled up my shirt. When she saw my stomach she began to cry too.

"Oh baby....this is joy! Why the tears? You should be happy!" "But Mama how can you say that I am only eighteen and I do not know who my baby's father is." My voice lowered to a whisper tone. "Mama there is something I did not tell you." Mama just stared at me. "Mama before I started dealing with Davon there was Dre." "The baby could be either one of theirs Mama!" "Look at me Stacie, I love you and things waaaaay worst than this done happened. I aint gon sit here and condemn, or look down on you for what you've done. Hell, I am glad we are where we are today. We can handle this together I promise. This could be a new beginning for both of us." Mama put a smile on my face and I sat down and let her blow dry my hair just like old times.

Mama had a series of questions and I answered them all. She liked Davon for the person that he was. She was grateful that Davon was there for me when she wasn't. However, after I told her everything bout Dre, she couldn't imagine why I left him in the first place. She thought I made a crazy decision not to move in with him. Once I explained to her how my past had a lot to do with the decisions I made she understood. I told her I saw how she did with my dad and I didn't want a man to have all control over me like that. And with Davon it was not like that. "Stacie I am soo sorry for the pain I caused you! I pray that one day you can forgive me." Mama said. She

Back then when I was twelve I couldn't wait to be eighteen. Now that I am eighteen it's not all that impressing to me. Finally my hair and all the food was done. Once Mama and I were dressed we played around the house and did a little fashion show. We trotted around in our panties, bras, and heels. Mama wasn't suppose to drink but I couldn't stop her. I have the faith in her that she wanted a better life. I prayed that it wouldn't be a set back for her. I had a glass of wine then we were off to the party. One of Mama's suga daddies picked us up. His name was Mr. Greg and by the look of things his money was very sweet. He drove a 2013 Cadillac Est. I think he did his own thing on the side if you know what I mean. I wasn't typically the show off type but I noticed certain things were changing about me.

I let Mama and Mr. Greg go in ahead of me. When they opened the door I could hear the music blasting Rick Ross. The music was just my cup of tea. I was a hip hop girl all day! My dress put me in the mind of something Tina Turner or my girl Beyoncé would've worn. Short and little. It was exactly that short and little. I covered my arms with my black leather waist length jacket. That night I turned it up a notch and wore my silver peep toe ankle boots. As usual my mushroom wrap was tight and my lip gloss was popping. Mama took it a step further and put me on some eye shadow and a little bit of lip liner. I looked gorgeous. I could have easily passed for 21 and older. I took a deep breath then entered the room.

It was more beautiful then, than it was before I left earlier. The light was dim and the candle lit centerpieces gave the room a touch of class. Walking in the room I smelled the aroma of the food Mama and Tionna cooked. I did not see Davon anywhere in sight. I was about to walk over to Tionna to ask her if she seen him and I felt someone come close behind me. The person wrapped their arms around me and their cologne began to turn me on. I prayed that it was Davon. The problem with that was Davon was not a cologne man. Whoever it was grinding behind me was about to get both our my Day. "Mmmm you smell good Boo!" "Thanks Sexy, you and my baby look good."

"Do we look good enough for you to never leave us?" "Hell yeah yall do! Stacie I love you girl!" I was too damn stunned to return the words! I did manage to give him an uncertain look. "Stacie I am for real I love you! Since you been in my life I sleep good at night. You gave me a reason to live again." "I want to do right by you and the baby." I was totally in awe, he almost had me in tears. Especially when I heard him say that him selling drugs was about to come to an end. When he said that the song came to an end. It was time to get our mingle on. I told Davon I loved him too, we kissed and then split for a bit.

The night was blissful and we had a good time. After two glasses of wine I turned down every other cup or glass that was past my way. Tionna came and brought along two females with her that I did not hang with. One of the chicks use to mess with Davon at one point but it was cool though. I could not bare being one of those insecure females. But I tell you what, trusting them was something I didn't plan on doing. When Davon saw my reaction to Tionna and her company he kissed up on me even more. He made sure whoever he slept with before me knew That I was the one now. My belly bulged out of my dress and I could hear one girl asking Tionna about me being pregnant. Mama and I were dancing at that time. She laughed and said my baby got some HATAS......HOLLA! We laughed and danced on. I chose to ignore it and party on.

I did not know how to take Tionna after that one. I decided to keep her close for sure! The party was about to come to an end, and I was more excited about the after party. I was suppose to call the dancer when I was ready for her so she could get ready and meet us there. When I pulled out my cell I noticed she had called three times. I immediately called back and told her it was almost time and I was sorry for missing her calls. She was cool about the whole deal, she wasn't in no rush.

breaking them. She felt like being with me that night was more important. Mama and I kissed and hugged, then me and Davon was on our way. We went to our room where the after party took place. This was something new for me, and I would be lying if I said I wasn't nervous.

Chapter Eight

had nothing to do with the room, it was all Davon's doing. He fixed it up with the rose pedals and candles. This might sound mean, but I wasn't impressed. I was grateful though. I know, that's mean but it is true. I mean watching movies and reading books tell you the same story about a mans idea of being romantic. The candles I love because there sensual, but the rose pedals I can do without. The long stem white roses are my kind. Davon stripped down to his boxers as soon as we hit the door. I didn't expect that at all. I still had a little bit more left up my sleeves before we got it on. I text the dancer and within five minutes there was a knock on the

"Room Service!" A woman's voice said. Davon can you get the door." "Yeah I got you......did you order something?" "No, I thought you did." Davon's face frowned. When he opened the door the stripper was standing there in her gear ready for action. Davon's tail was hilarious. I could hear Davon proclaiming to the dancer that she had the wrong room. She assured him she didn't. I heard her ask him was his name Davon. Then his punk ass started whispering. "Yeah but I don't know you and you about to get me killed lady!" I chuckled under my breath and tried to act like I was doing something in the room. I knocked down the cd rack to distract Davon from the door and it worked like a charm.

When he heard the impact he turned around to see if I was okay. "Baby you good!" By the time he went to go back to the door the my mouth dropped. "What the hell!" Were the words that came out of my mouth. "Baby I know what this look like..... I...I don't know her ass!" Davon said stuttering. Once he shut up I was able to finish my sentence. "What the hell took you so long!" I said smiling. Then there went Davon's mouth to the floor.

The mood was awesome, as his body relaxed his man muscle grew. Hello Stacie, the stripper said in her sexy voice. "Hello to you too Candy!" Need I say more! The chick was bad, she did her thing too. It was like watching real live porn. I think if I wasn't pregnant I would have experienced my first threesome. By the end of the night Davon was satisfied which made me satisfied too. He could not believe I engaged in such sexual content. I admit, it was different but hell of fun! Davon made love to me sooo good that night! He took his time, he aimed to please and he even got in touch with his emotional side a bit. Now that made me impressed with him! After we shared great sex we ended the night with some good old hog calling sleep. The next morning mama called my phone waking us up. I picked up the phone to hear her loud voice in my ear.

"Girl I had a good dam time last night! Thank you boo for helping me see what's good in life. Stacie I love you baby!" "Mama I love you too! You had a good time and I am glad, but back to business tomorrow right Mama." "No Diggidy No Doubt!" "Oooh Mama you a clown!" We both laughed. "I had fun too Mama, love you." "Aight Stase I'm on my way back in I'll call you later."

When I turned over on the bed Davon put his ear to my belly and started talking to the baby. "I love you Day." "I love you too Stacie. What would you think if I tell you I'm gonna sign up to take my GED tomorrow." "OMG!..What do I think? I think that is perfect!" I said. I was ecstatic that he was for real about doing right. Check out time was at 12 noon but we left around 11:30. Back to business for us. We hadn't left the hotel yet and Davon had already had three sales. He promised that after he finished he would be right home.

out of my mouth. I did have some type of feelings for Davon but I wasn't sure if it was love or not. Not to mention Dre was always on my mind. My mind wouldn't let me forget how young I was and where I had come from. As I acknowledged where I was, I was very thankful, but where I was going had to become clear.

I think it was more of me feeling sorry for him when I found out his life's story. I thought my life was bad, seems like his was worse. The feelings were mutual between us and we were both trying to move on from our past. He forgave me for busting his head and he was willing to accept all my baggage. Maybe there is a deeper connection. Davon also had a way with the ladies, he was surely a ladies man. At first I wouldn't believe it if I saw it, and now I was falling victim to it. I wouldn't put Davon in the saint category nor would I say he has not stepped out on me. But what I will say is this, he show me mad respect. After all the negativity, I was looking for something like a positive outcome. Even though things started going right in my life I still wasn't sold. After all I didn't go to my appointment yet and I was a drug dealer. Anything could happen!

Chapter Nine

Gracefully we had a busy day ahead of us, and it was one that I was looking forward too. It was Monday February the 9th and I had a scheduled doctors appointment. After the appointment Davon and I had plans to go enroll himself in a GED program. Then thereafter we both were going to fill out some applications. Besides doing hair I didn't know how to do much. It was so uplifting getting on the right track. The appointment was set for nine that morning. Today we would get clarified confirmation from the doctor about the pregnancy. Knowing I was pregnant was one thing but I wanted to know were me and the baby healthy. They would be able to tell me how far along I was and some more. It was just my luck, my cousin Shalese called my phone just as Davon and I walked in the clinic. I was excited to talk to her but there also was a lot of info that I was holding out on. What a catastrophe! When I answered the phone the first thing that came out her mouth was.

"Hey cuz where are you?" "On my way to the clinic wussup with you?" "Wai....wait, what did you say Stacie?" "You never go get a check up what is going on with you cuz?" My lips were clinched tight. "Wow Lese, I'll have to explain a little later I am at the clinics door. I'll call you back I promise!" "Ok." Shalese sighed. After that conversation I felt horrible.

After that, I knew that was another thing that would have to change! Davon would just have to forgive Shalese and move on. She will always be my cousin, that right there was enough to make me feel hear my name. "Coming here for a pregnancy test isn't appealing, so I darn sure am not coming back for prenatal care." I told Davon. The wait was long, They were short of staff and I could not begin to utter the words on how unprofessional they were! Ghetto chicks with long finger nails, big hoop earrings and the smacking of gum! I was disgusted!

Finally they called my name and Davon and I went to the back. The doctor gave me a cup to pee in and showed me where the bathroom was at. The results were positive, which we already knew. The doctor gave me a sonogram and performed a pelvic exam. She asked me when was my last menstral and I said about two months ago. After she did the pelvic exam she said her findings contradicted my last menstrual date. She said it was either a big baby or I was carrying twins. My uterus was measuring eighteen weeks. That would make me four and a half months. That was shocking! Ok.......if she said two and a half three months that would of been more believable. But, was I carrying a baby that long and did not know? Thinking back that far, I couldn't remember almost five months of symptoms.

Maybe the weight gaining, but four and a half months. While she was doing the sonogram I laid there emotionless. My face was blank and I had no words to say. Davon had such a cache smile on his. Those grillz in his mouth lit up the room. When I realize he didn't pay attention to the time frame I began to wonder did he even care of the possibility. I thought he was dumb, naive, or just plain stupid. For about a month or so I was sleeping with him and Dre and he knew it. Oh well if he was willing to be here, we will accept him with open arms. A feeling of relief came over me. The doctor asked us if we wanted to know the sex of the baby and I declined. However, Davon wanted to know. I somehow persuaded him into waiting so we could find out together when I deliver.

Nervous was my first feeling, but now I have to admit to being anxious. I couldn't wait until the baby was born. Leaving the clinic, making a few phone calls later on when I was alone. I knew I didn't owe Dre any explanation but I thought it was only right I did what was best in this situation. There was going to be a baby involved in my life soon. My cousin was on my mind heavy, but Dre seemed to be even more. This could damn well be his seed. I then realized how heart crushing that could leave Davon. What was I suppose to do? It's amazing where the paths in life will take you. I would always joke around with Shalese about her dirt catching up with her, and now look at me.

I guess mine caught up with me first. We drove to the GED office on Baltimore St. where Davon registered for his classes. There were several different classes he had to choose from. The program was designed to fit many different needs. One program was for six weeks, then there was one for three months and another one for six months. Don't ask me what the hurry was with Davon, because I was shocked when he chose the six week program. It was like he was in a rush for everything at that point. They scheduled him for a pre test and we were on our way. So far our day was pretty productive like anticipated. After that we went off to job hunt. By the time we handled the GED business I had a taste for a slice of pizza and a chili cheese dog.

After I ate I got a bad case of nigga-Itis. Just as I was about to ask Davon to take a rein check on job hunting, I spotted this huge sign in the window of a hair salon. The salon was located on park Avenue. "Davon pull over please!" "You aright?" Davon asked. "Yeah I'm good, I want to run in this salon and see exactly what are they hiring for." "Oh shux baby abouta bust dey heads huh!" "Boy you so stupid!" As I got out the car I heard him still cackling, I just slammed the door. "What a freaking fool he is!" I said to myself. The hair salon was lovely, inside was painted different shades of purple with silver fixtures. "Hi you doing my name is Stacie, I noticed your hiring sign in the window."

shampoo girls and a stylist." "Can I apply for the stylist position?"
"Sure but we don't do paper apps, it's all hands on. When can I see
your work?" "Any day besides today is good, frankly the evenings
are good for me though." "Honey round here we do everything in
the morning!" "Oh dag, well ok I still have school during the day. I
was out today because of a clinic appointment." "What did you say
your name was again?" "I am Stacie." "Stacie I guess I can a bend
the rules a little bit. I like that you want to work already! What the
hell it's my shop!" My eyes grew wider and I instantly smiled. She
told me to handle my business for the rest of the week then come see
her Friday straight after school. Once was a girl with no direction
looking at life now I practically knew every move I wanted to make.

When I went back to the car Davon still cheesing, showing them
ugly grills. This time I was cheesing right back at him! "So what
happened?" "She told me to come back Friday to apply for the stylist
position." "Why you couldn't apply now?" "Well because I have to
show her my skills first, it's hands on only." "Oh aight." "I have to
come straight after school, is it okay if you bring me?" "If you can't
I can catch the bus." "Now you know I'll bring you, stop playing wit
me girl!" Both of us laughed. "Day I love you but can we take a rein
check and do the job hunting another day this week?"

"Hell yeah that is fine with me! Do you want me to take you home
Stase?" "Yes please." I replied. After that there was a moment of
silence. Davon turned the music up and I went on daydreaming.
Dre was on my mind nonstop! True he did me dirty.....but he also
left a hell of an impression on me! Then I have to mention again,
that this baby might be his! I don't know what it was with Dre, but
I do not think he completely let go either. What other reason could
there be for him to keep paying the cell phone bill. I have not talked
to him in a few months, and me calling him now would be a little
strange I thought. I couldn't live in such a lie. He deserve to know
the truth one way or another. I had no problem with taking a DNA
test. Those were all the thoughts that filled my brain on the ride

Once I was inside the apartment I straight kicked off my shoes. There I sat on the couch feeling mad confused. "Screw it!" I said aloud. I called Dre, I had no clue as to what I would say. He did call me on my birthday so I'll use that as the excuse to call him back. "Hello." Dre answered. "Hi Dre are you busy?" I asked. "Not really, what's good! I called you to wish you a happy birthday." "Yeah I know that is why I am calling you back." "Oh really, three days later Stacie! So what we can't be friends?" Dre said arrogantly, but with care still in his voice.

"Dre you hurt me! What the hell do you really expect from me!" "Stacie like I told you before I am sorry. I can't take it back but I would love to fix it." "Dre it's little to late for that!" "Dre so many things have changed in my life since us!" "Right now Dre I am involved with someone and so are you." "Stacie it's not like dat, when me and you were dealing with each other I did everything in my power to cut all tides with her. I have to keep it real Stacie, you aint make it no easier for me." "That's why I asked you to come stay with me, because she is like a bad habit I can't get rid of!" "Excuse me!" "So basically you were using me to get over your ex!" "So what you're saying is she got your ass addicted, nose wide the heck open huh! I don't know why I bothered calling your behind!" In a stern voice he demanded me to listen.

"Stacie I've been with her since I was fifteen and that is along time for me. I never meant to hurt you. All I know is she is not the woman for me. I admit I screwed up but I know if you were there things would of been way different." I sat on the phone and became real emotional. Listening was all I could do. "Stacie are you still there?" "Yes I am here." I said with sadness in my voice. "Are you crying, please don't cry! I am so sorry Stacie!" "Dre it's okay but I need to see you, I have something important I need to tell you." "Ok when." "Dre said. "Dre this is serious!" "Okay Stase, I said when." "Maybe tomorrow, I'm a little beat I had a busy day." "Alright then, call me please." "Yeah I'll be sure too."

I heard a loud boom. It startled the hell out of me! Before I could react I needed to know what in the world was going on. It sounded like the apartment complex main door. When I looked out of the window I noticed Davon's car parked crooked in the parking lot. My body quickly woke up then! His car was in the lot but he was not there. I said to myself. Oh goodness is somebody chasing him! I ran to the door and he was darting up the steps.

"Go in the house Stacie!" He was out of breath and his jeans were torn. "What is going on Davon!" He swiftly ran past me and went up in the closet and grabbed the gun. When I saw the gun I was scared speechless! I yelled his name. "Davon!" He started mumbling something and all I heard was, "Dem niggas wanna shoot at me! Imma killem, Imma killem!" "Davon you need to talk to me, who was shooting at you?" Although he never gave me an answer I was able to calm him down. The next thing I was concerned about was did they know where we lived at. He said no, I hoped he was right. It seemed like from that day forward things started going down hill for me and Davon's work on the street. The next week Davon was arrested for a handgun. The house where he kept his stash got raided. Initially, once we had confirmation I was pregnant we no longer kept the drugs in the house.

After the raid our supplies became very limited. Davon and Kalief had a huge fall out. Which I knew was coming but Day wasn't trying to hear it! Davon stayed in the house more then, but there was the stress about the bills getting paid. I did end up getting the job at the salon, I just stayed too sick to work. She agreed to rehire me after the baby was born. I began to feel sorry for Davon again. It was like once he realized it was time for a change and put his first foot forward everything went haywire. He was unable to focus on the pre GED test so he failed. No jobs were trying to hire him because of the recent hand gun charge. The Davon that I could not stand appeared right before my eyes. The Davon that I first met, the one that looked

Chapter Nine

like he belonged to the wolf family. Our future was looking very gloomy and at that point there was not an option.

I called Dre up and told him to pick me up from school. Unlike Day, Dre was very reliable. Dude would be outside the school before school even let out. He would never keep me waiting. Now Day.......
I could tell him 12 and he would be there by 1. I was now six months and Dre still had no clue. Yeah me calling him the next day, huh I never did it! He had not seen me since the end of October it was now the end of march. I could see his facial expression as I was going toward the car. My face was glowing, my nose had spread across my face and my hair grew to it's fullest potential.

The legs that use to be bony were now thick and pretty. My belly is what took the cake. It was waaaaaaay out there! I was huge but beautiful. I was approaching his car from the drivers side. So when I saw his mouth drop in his lap I smiled and told him to pick up his mouth. He unlocked the door and I slowly sat down in the front seat. "I'm getting punked right!" I laughed so hard my bladder instantly filled up. "No Dre you're not getting punked!" "Dam Stacie how you gon do me like this!" "Do you like what Dre?" "You went and got pregnant on me! You know how bad I want a kid but you go give another dude a baby!" "Look Dre be careful what you ask for! This baby that I am carrying could darn well be your baby! I honestly don't know who the baby's father is. It's between you and my boyfriend." "How many months are you?" "Uhhh six!" "For real!" "Yup for real!"

He really started feeling bad then because he blamed himself for not being there for me. Like his old self he slapped two hundred dollar bills in my hand and asked me was that enough until next week. I gave him the money right back. He insisted and then put it in my coat pocket. I told Dre everything, and I mean everything. How I lied about going to stay with my mom. I explained to him that she was on drugs real bad at that time. I also told him that I was more embarrassed to talk to him but it came more natural talking to Davon.

relate without judging me. I even told him about Cal's situation and he was shocked. "Stacie can I have a kiss?" "Nope!" I wanted to so bad! "Please can I kiss those soft lips!" I teased him, puckered, and licked my lips before I laid a delicious wet one on him. When I pulled back, he was still there in the kissing position gazing in my eyes. Before I knew it, we were riding to his apartment. I missed him and it showed. I dropped my panties as soon as I hit the door.

The love making we experienced was oh so sensual. He took his time with me and it felt so good. Remembering the love we made before, I was falling for him all over again. Suddenly Davon's face flashed in my head. "Oh my gracious what am I doing!" It felt so good, I wasn't about to stop. After I was done Dre asked me was I sure I wanted to go back. "Hell yeah I'm sure!" "Stacie how am I spose to live with the fact that the baby could be mine?" I spoke in a soft tone. "Dre when I have the baby we will get a test done, ok." "But Stacie I would like to know how you are doing. I don't want to miss out on this experience. Specially if the baby is mine." "Dre I do understand that and it will not be a problem if we keep in touch but you and I both know there is some things we have to take care of first.

"Oh yeah what about your girl?" "Man I'll drop her like hot water for you!" "See that is exactly what I mean, you tryna start something else before you are even done with what you have! Take me home!" "What, did I say something wrong?" "Dre you know what I don't get though, it was only like a month and you stepped out on me so what makes you so sure now?" "I know Stacie it's a long story and whenever you are willing to listen I'll tell you all about it ." "Aright for now we'll just have to take things one day at a time. I had to admit I still had feelings for Dre so I was no better than him.

Dre drove me to Tionna's house. The vibe between her and I was unexplainable. The atmosphere was dreadful. Tionna did not have too much to say. Once I noticed the mood wasn't right I text Davon.

catcher was, this dude only had on a tank top and a pair of boxers! Ohhh, so this is why I am getting the silent treatment! I said to myself. I never made it apparent to Tionna that I did not like Kalief, but I'm pretty sure he did. Not even waiting for Davon to text back I dipped off. I prayed he call back soon because I wasn't fitting to stand on the dag on bus stop. When I wobbled around the corner I spotted Davon's car. The windows were foggy so my sight wasn't clear at all. I couldn't believe his dumb self, sitting in the car smoking!

Then he was not aware of his surroundings. Those same dudes could of came back and killed him! I was pissed! He dammmn sure couldn't afford to go back to jail. My first intentions were to go pull the door open because he never locked the door. Then I decided not too, because it would be my own fault if he shot me out of fear. Since the incident with him getting shot at, he carried his piece everywhere. I stood there and contemplated for a half a second. The windows started clearing up and by then I was getting suspicious. I could tell he had just turned on the defoggers. It don't take a rocket scientist to know when something fishy is going on. I saw Davon and his lips were moving like he was having a conversation. However, I saw no phone near his ear.

"Oh no screw that!" That was my que! This bastard better have an explanation why the hell he didn't text me back! I said to myself. I felt the butterflies regroup in my stomach as I got closer. Then I felt the baby ball up with every step I took. I made my way over to the car. I am far from a dummy so I went to the passenger side. Like I thought the car door was unlocked. When I swung the car door open I made a shocking discovery! This no good bastard was getting his man muscle sucked. The broad lifted her head up so fast, and as fast as she lifted up was as fast as I socked her trifling ass! I don't know where I got the strength from, but I grabbed her by the hair and swung dat ass out of the car. I had forgot all about me being pregnant.

the car and guess what, he came to my rescue. He wasn't about to be no super hero of mine, I banged him too! "So dis what the heck you do when I am not around! Yoose a dumb lame ass nigga!" I went on and on and on. I said so much stuff I hurt them feelings. Like a man, he couldn't take the trash talking so he call himself jacking me up. That's when I heard Tionna's mouth.

"Get the hell off of her!" She told Davon how trifling he was. I refused to go with Davon so I went back around Tionna's house to get myself together. By the time we got back there Kalief had left so I was a lot more comfortable. Tionna told me that was why she was acting all weird before. Davon had the audacity to knock on her door to see if she had any condoms. Once he saw Kalief in there he rolled out. "Stacie I didn't know how to tell you that, plus you're pregnant! You do not need all of that drama!" "Stase I am sorry!" Tionna went on to tell me how Davon was like a brother to her. Ultimately she didn't want to betray his trust. She said she felt bad how things were turning out. Not only for me and Davon, but for him and Kalief as well. When I came through, the moment was more awkward because she said she just got finish checking Kalief's butt.

I was shocked that Tionna said after that day they wouldn't be seeing each other anymore. In my opinion Kalief didn't give a care, he was using her anyway! I was glad Tionna came to her senses and it was time for me to come to mine. I laughed when I thought about me actually out there fighting! It wasn't a damn thing funny about me being out there fighting! I figured it was the power of some good ole wood. Davon was very blessed. It's true he had size and capacity over Dre, but Dre always aimed to please me. In turn it made the sex always pleasurable. I didn't tell Tionna my plans but I told her I had to hurry and take care of something. At first I was going to call Dre back, then I said no way! I didn't want my bookie involved in the chaos. Instead I caught a hack straight to the apartment.

ram sacking it, I called the maintenance men and ask them could they come change the locks. I told them I had a very jealous boyfriend and him and I had a fight. I told them I was scared he was gonna come back. I lied and told them that he had threatened me. I planned to go to the police station and file a complaint but for now I needed my locks changed. They didn't give me any grief at all they just changed the locks. I was so happy when I thought back to signing the lease, I put him nowhere on it! After they changed the locks they went on their merry way.

Now let's see what that dummy do! I could not wait to see the look on his face. I just hope he don't do anything stupid. Better believe the police would be on speed dial. He should know what is good for him and stay away. I had to get my thoughts together before I did something on impulse. I practically had already made up my mind. Which was that I didn't want to be with his tail anymore! Our timing was pretty intriguing if you ask me. Dre dropped me off after our little rendezvous, and I just so happen to catch Davon in his. That might seem a little strange, but it wasn't the fact that he was screwing around! It was the point that I caught him, and where he was that made it that much more disgusting. It was nothing he could tell me! And did I feel bad, hell no, because the bastard did not catch me!

After playing the tough tony roll I cried like a baby. I started having feelings of not being good enough. All the facts began to over shadow my thoughts. Both guys that I slept with cheated on me. In Dre's case I can't really say he cheated he just wasn't totally honest. However, Davon and I, we did become exclusive to one another. The fool even told me that he loved me. I suppose, instead of beating myself up I could say, what comes around goes around. Looking at both situations I wasn't no saint. No matter what I did I could not express my feelings. It was a must that I man up, or should I say woman up, I couldn't run forever! At that point the urge for me to talk to someone became urgent. The first person that popped into my mind was Shalese.

in months. I couldn't explain why my heart was pounding while I dialed her number. Once again I had to pull myself together. "OMG!" Shalese said when she picked up the phone. My heart was still pounding. For a few seconds I sat on the phone not saying a word. "Uuuuuhh, HELLO!" "Hey Lese it's me." I said in a sad tone. "Stacie what is wrong?" "Lese there is a lot that is wrong, and there's something I need to tell you." "Shalese I pray you can forgive me for what I did!" "Stase please don't tell me you slept with Gerome!" "No, no, no Lese!" That's when the silence fell upon me again. "Hey Stacie whateva it is I am pretty sure we can work it out so just spit it out!" "I slept with Davon." I said in the lowest tone possible. Shalese did not react like I thought she was.

"Girl...........you thought I was gonna be mad at you for that!" "Yeah!" I replied. "But Shalese that is just the beginning!" "Talk to me Stase, I am your cousin that's what I'm here for." "Shalese I'm six months pregnant and I don't know if the baby belongs to Dre or Davon. To make a long story short me and Davon became buddies the day your father came and moved everything out. Davon helped me break the pad lock off the door and things grew from there. Dre went back to his ex because I wouldn't move in with him. Lese I've been wanting to talk to you about this but I didn't know how. I know I'm a fool right! Just say it I won't be mad!"

"No cousin I won't, just tell me the rest." Shalese said. "Since then Davon and I moved in an apartment together. Before today things were okay. Not to long ago I caught him getting head from some broad in his car." "Dam that nigga aint change a bit!" Shalese replied. "I'm sorry you had to go through that Stase. You know what though, I'm not trying to sound petty or nothing but I wish you did trust me enough to tell me. I would of told you all about his trifling butt! So what now Stacie? " "I don't know!" Shalese and I chatted a little while longer then mama beeped in. Before I got off of the phone with Shalese we made plans to catch a movie that weekend. Mama didn't want much. But the way I was feeling I did not want her to took my sleepy butt to bed.

"Boom...Boom... Boom!" The startling sound of fist pounding on the door woke me straight out of my sleep. "That bastard! "It was three forty five in the morning. I couldn't believe that guy, after all these hours he was just making an attempt to come home and fix things! He didn't try calling, apologizing, or nothing! "He must be stupid if he think it's this easy!" I said to myself. "Who is it?" Of course I knew who it was, I just wanted to hear him squirm! "It's me open the door!" "Hell no, and you better go about your dam business before I call the police!" I could not believe that I was living that moment. Hidden Resentment, Bolding Page/ 118

"So this is how you gon do me!" "Yup, now go bout your dam business!" "Aight den!" Davon said. Then he took off toward the steps. Whatever that was it did not ease my mind not one bit! For one, he never apologized, and then he walked away that much easier. No I didn't think our relationship was going to be peaches and cream, but I did not picture that either. Falling back to sleep was so hard for me. It was almost impossible! I tossed and turned and could not seem to get comfortable. Even though I was hurt, I was also more determined than ever. My baby was who I had to live for then. Thinking about my mama's progress also had me motivated. My mother had been through hell and back and she was still here fighting. I wasn't about to let something this surreal ruin my peace of mind. Mama promised to make it up by being a better grandmother to my baby than she was a mother to me. Mama disappointed me a lot in the past, but for some reason this time I felt the truth coming from her heart. I think Aunt Tina's death really did a number on

Chapter Ten

The next morning on my way to school, I was a wreck! Being tired was an understatement. I couldn't believe how fatigue I was. The twenty-three bus went from my apartment to Edmondson Ave. The further along I got in my pregnancy the more miserable the bus ride became. It seemed so much longer than normal. I would get nauseous and dizzy because of the bumpy roller coaster ride. Being young and pregnant was not unheard of but it darn sure was popular either. The other students would talk smack about me. The boys would go out of their way to make perverted comments to me, and the teachers they gave me dirty looks like I was contagious. There was one time when the guidance counselor suggested I go to the all girl pregnant school on my side of town. She claim it would be much easier on me being closer to my house and all. She told me that her job was to look out for my best interest. I let everything she said roll off my back. At first I believed she was being nosy and wanted me out of the school. It's funny now though, because I only gave what she said a second thought when I felt like I was about to puke out the bus window. Maybe she was right, it would have been in my best interest to go there.

Ready for anything was my attitude that morning going into the school building. First I had to shake the queasy feeling and I would be good. So far so good, Davon hadn't crossed my mind either. Well, maybe a little! Before I could sit down in my seat, my homeroom algebra teacher pulled me in the hallway. She pulled an envelope from a folder with my name on it. I had the look of confusion written all over my face. Ms. Armstrong read my face all to well because the first thing she said was, "It's not bad news don't worry. "Then my whole demeanor reluctantly changed. The letter was a decision to test me and put me in my correct grade. I was happy as hell! Ms. Armstrong sent me to the third floor with the letter so I could take the exam. The exam was an all day process. I had to test out of a few classes that I didn't take. Surprisingly the exams weren't that hard.

Dre text me while I was in last period. He asked me was I okay. I told Dre to come get me from school, praying Davon didn't show up. He said ok and that was that. After all the exams I was so exhausted. When the bell rung my pregnant behind was the first one up. Leaving out the class I called mama. She laughed at me so hard, because I sounded like I was out of breath walking and talking. I told her it wasn't funny and that I've been feeling bad all day. I mentioned the pregnant school to her and she told me that is where she went to school when she was pregnant with me. Mama had my back on whatever it was I wanted to do.

Before I could make a move, getting my results were my first priority. If I passed they would put me in the eleventh grade. I couldn't ask for anything more. With everything going on with me I told mama going to the pregnant school might be the best thing. Then the second surprise of the day happened. Mama came out her mouth, and said, "Stacie let me know so I can take You," I don't know if surprise was the right word, but I was very shocked!

When I spotted Dre's car coming across the lot I told her I was going to call her when I got home. Dre saw me and started smiling from ear to ear. As I caught his eyes I peeped Davon's car coming down the Avenue. The penguin walk became the racing penguin walk. The baby was becoming more heavy on my bladder the faster I walked. I felt like I had to pee and some more mess. Dre sat there laughing his tail off, not even knowing what was happening. "Dag girl what's up?" "Why you walking so fast?" "Haha Dre, very funny, I gotta pee!" "Why didn't you go to the bathroom in the school

Chapter Ten

building?" "I did about twenty minutes ago." I said lying. "Did you eat?" Dre asked. "Earlier, let's go get something." "I already know honey." I looked at him, smiled and rolled my eyes. Thinking to myself how I just dodged a bullet, I burst out laughing. About fifteen minutes had gone by and my phone started vibrating. When I looked and saw it was Davon I rejected it. He called again and I rejected it again.

The third time Davon called, Dre noticed what was going on. "Trouble in paradise, Stacie!" Dre said. "Whateva you say Dre, paradise are your words not mine!" I planned on making Davon sweat. I wasn't letting him slide that easy. Eventually he would have to get some of his stuff from the house but it would be on my time. The times when I did think about him I pictured that nasty tramp sucking his pickle. Dre took me to the Hibachi Grill and we enjoyed the perks of all you can eat for ten dollars. While we sat there and talked I made it very clear that I wasn't up for any detours. I told him I needed to go straight home.

"Stacie can I tell you something in confidence?" "Sure wussup, anyway who the hell am I going to tell!" "Ok smarty, but all jokes aside. Stacie it's real hard for me to be alone. I feel like I am dependent on a female." "Honestly Dre I can some what see that. Why do you think you are like that?" "I don't know but since I was a young boy I always had a girl in my life. Trina has done everything under the sun to me and I continued to stay there and put up with it. "Oh Trina's her name huh!" I said. "You didn't know that?" I just cut my eye at him. "And how was I suppose to know that Dre! You trying it are you!" After the oh shit look, he then went on and continued to tell me that she stabbed him, cheated on him, and practically used him for his money. I thought to myself, you just a damn dummy. "Well I hope things get better for you and her. "Stacie that is not what I want to hear!"

"Why not me and you?" As much as I wanted him, I was tired of the back and forth. "Let me think about it." "Oh so now you're gonna consider it! Yesterday you was telling me I was too late, what happened

I said. "When I said there was trouble in paradise!" I said, nothing but my eyes always told Dre my story. I tried hard to fight back my tears but they came pouring. I hated the emotional pregnant crap, I couldn't control my emotions for nothing. "What the hell! Stacie did I say something wrong?" "No!" I said sobbing. "You actually said something right! Yesterday I saw Davon cheating on me when you dropped me off." "I don't want this to sound mean Stase but we had great sex yesterday too! You remember don't you?" "Yeah Dre but we didn't get caught. He aint fucking catch me sucking your dick, did he!" I snapped. He hugged me and apologized. "Stacie if you need to talk I am all ears." "No I'm good, I guess I'm just pissed cause once again Stacie gets inconvenienced." "Stacie you know I offered you a place to stay, but now I am wondering if I would have said that we would be together, would things have been different." "Look Dre I can't change what has happened." "You're right so let's drop it, but first Stacie I wanna know can we work things out and start fresh?" "Dre it would be unfair to emphasize on that right now when we don't even know if you're the baby's father." "That is sort of the point with all things to consider, don't you think the universe could be sending us a sign. We belong together girl!"

"It don't matter I just want to be there for you and the baby!" Dre and I talked a little while longer then he dropped me off, this time in front of the apartment building. I was happy to be home about to take my daily nap. My phone read two voicemails. "Please enter your access code then press pound." "Stacie it's me Davon I know I messed up........ I'm so sorry. I hope you can forgive me. Tell me what I can do to fix it, call me back! I left this morning so fast so I wouldn't stress you and my baby out. I love you! I understand if you need some time and space, but I need to get a few things from the apartment. Please call me back I love you Baby!" "Ha, really!" I said. I ignored Davon's message and prepared for my nap. My nap was very important to me. Off to la la land I went.

ever possible, knowing Davon had not heard from me yet. My cell phone started ringing off the hook. I was in the living room and my cell was in the bedroom on the nightstand. For a while I brushed it off thinking it was Davon calling back being a nuisance. When I realized whoever it was wasn't going to stop calling until I answered it, I went and got it. I went into a cold frenzy when I saw that it was Tionna calling me all those times. That was strange activity for her. She would call once and if she got no answer than that was what it was. And if it was important she would just leave a message. "Oh my goodness!" I called Tionna's phone back but she was out of the service area.

My worrying became more apparent, I couldn't hide it. Yes I was truly mad at Davon but he could still be my Baby's father. I wasn't that mad at him that I wanted something to happen to him. I finally got through to Tionna, but when I did I could barely understand anything she was saying. What I did hear frightened the heck out of me. I was no more good. Tionna was talking so fast but when I heard Davon's name I listened extra hard. "Stacie I didn't know......I didn't know! I thought he was cool Stacie! Day..... Davon and Kalief was fighting and Kalief pulled a gun out on Day. When he tried to shoot him the gun jammed. Kalief was behind all of it, dem... dem nigga's shooting at Davon and all. Stacie, Davon told me about you not wanting to talk to him. Please Stacie I am begging you, put it aside for a minute because somebody is gonna get hurt. Davon is pissed and he needs you. Plus Kalief threatened you Stacie and Davon went off, So please be careful Stase. Stacie I'm really afraid for Davon call him."

Through out the entire phone conversation I didn't get in one word. Tionna was devastated, I could hear Miss Charlotte telling Tionna to calm down. That was Tionna's mother. After she spilled the bad news the call dropped. My heart became real soft and weak and felt like it dropped too. My thoughts drove me crazy, they were speeding sixty miles per hour. My instincts kicked in and I called Davon's ten minutes of me calling I didn't know what to think. Every time things would pick up and change for the better in my life something horrible would happen to take my peace of mind. I was pregnant with my baby and I looked forward to happy days. Mama turned her life around tremendously and was due to come home to her own place in about three weeks. Then there was my schooling, and I have to say things were coming along great there. My confidence finally did a one eighty and my bony behind finally gained some weight. For every good thing I mentioned a bad thing happened plus some. My circle wasn't big so most of the time when I needed someone to talk to it would be Shalese, Lisa, or Tionna. I couldn't call mama with all the madness because I needed her to focus on getting herself together. I wanted her to have a speedy recovery. She would be filled in on all the dirt when she came home. Tionna was a mess and I damn sure was not calling Dre with that madness.

Chapter Eleven

tried waiting it out but the wait was killing me. That bastard Kalief, I knew he wasn't right! A snake couldn't really describe who he really was. I wish Davon would have listened to me. And why is my name coming out of his nasty mouth! I thought. I cringed with the thought of it. After that there was no way in hell Davon could still consider him a friend. With the stressing and worrying I began to feel sick. I grabbed a glass and got the milk out the fridge. As my body became weaker my hands started trembling out of control. I tried to control my hands from trembling but they just trembled even harder. A lot of the milk didn't make it into the glass, I spilled milk all over the place. Every time I stressed, so did the baby. I figured the milk would put a coating on my stomach until I ate. Picking up my phone a weird feeling came over me double time. The street life was some unpredictable mess. It wasn't like I could pick up the phone and call 911. What was I suppose to say? "Shoot!" I Felt so helpless. Instead of being scared I became angry. Something told me to get out of the apartment, and I brushed that feeling off. I figured the safest place for me at that time was my own home.

I dialed Davon's phone again that time I had to leave a message. I wanted him to know how much I really cared about him in spite of the recent events. No matter how upset I was I wanted him to come home off of the streets. Regardless of everything, I truly did still have feelings for him. Secondly, I needed to know what could I do to help. Most of all, I wanted to know where he was at. "Leave me your about everything just come home sweetie!" Then there was a loud bang on the door. "Dag that was fast, I'm on my way to the door." I hung up the phone and headed to the door. I was so happy to see that Davon was okay. If only that were the case!

I swung the door open with all of my emotions pouring out. Before I could retract and close the door it was too late. "DAMN!" I let it in! It was the snake..........he swiveled his way into my house. Like a thief in the night there he was. Pulling a 45 caliber out of his dip, my life flashed before my eyes. "What do you want, Davon aint here!" I screamed. "Shut up whore, I know Davon aint here!...........It's you I'm looking for!" "What I do to you?" I said, still trying to play it cool. I tried to play like I didn't know anything! He wasn't buying it at all. "Please Kalief don't hurt me and the baby!" "SHUT UP BITCH! Kalief screamed. "All this, this bullshit dats going on is because of you! Davon use to be my boy, he met yo ass and that was it for us!" Kalief grabbed me by my hair and yanked me onto the sofa. I cried out, please, "God help me!"

"Didn't I say shut the fuck up! You gon give me some of dat pussy! C'mon show me how you did it, how you turn my boy against me? Is it really that good?" "What.....what are you talking about Kalief ?" "You are a sick bastard!" I shouted. Kalief started snatching on my robe trying to get it off. My mind began to play tricks on me. I thought I heard my unborn child crying. I started fighting back. Screaming, kicking, and yelling! "Get the fuck off of me!" I knew it was coming but I didn't see it. Kalief took the butt of the gun and pistol whipped me on the side of my head. I could hear him, and I could feel him. However, the impact of the gun interfered with my eyesight so I could no longer see him. After the last blow my body fell limp. I could feel the tears falling down my face as I gave up hope for me and my baby. There was no way he was going to let us stay and out I was dying. He put a 45 in my butt and jammed it back and forth. Never had anything entered my world so violent. I screamed so loud and my crying became uncontrollable. I was in agony, trying to handle the excruciating pain. He took the gun out and he stuck his penis in the same. It was at that moment that I didn't want to live anymore. My body went into a convulsion, I began to spaz and shake. Kalief's voice felt like a knife gutting me like a fish. "Now how it feel to have something taken huh! Don't worry Imma put choo outta ya misery soon!" He rammed his penis in me so hard I vomited all over myself and the sofa. I felt like God had forsaken me, and this time for good.

"You nasty trick I should kill you for that shit!" As he came closer to put his penis back inside of me I spit in his face. I knew I was gonna die anyway so I wanted him to really know how I felt about him. He damn near beat the life out of me! Pregnant and all I was trying to escape. My face and head was so swollen I could barely lift it. Once Kalief realized things were getting out of control he tried to shut me up by choking me. He choked me until I was damn near was on my last breath. There was no more air for me to breath. I didn't understand why I was still alive. Physically I couldn't say anything but my inner spirit cried and fought. " God why is this happening to me? Please God help me, us. It's two of us Lord, and the baby is pure, cover us in the blood of your son." I mentally prayed.

As I laid there helpless I heard the hinges on the front door. The sound was oh so familiar. Kalief wasn't familiar with it but I knew someone else had come in. That's when I heard Davon's voice. Under any other circumstances I would have been happy to hear his voice. But this time the feeling of fear over powered me. Davon couldn't believe his eyes, what he saw must of cut a deep wound. The anger and desperation in his voice told me his eyes were watery. "Get off of her man! C'mon man, why you doing this? Dis between me and you dog, let her go! Please, please man." When please came from Davon's lips I knew it was over for both of us. "Davon what choo

The room fell silent and the floor beside me shook. Kalief was still on the floor straddled over me, so it had to be Davon lunging at Kalief. Kalief took his hands from around my neck then I heard the shot. It was one shot. It was loud, it was frightening, and I didn't know who caught it! Kalief's body was no longer on top of me. When I heard the footsteps and felt the floor vibrate I let out a sigh of relief. I was glad Davon came to save me. When I realized the footsteps went toward the front door I was puzzled. By my sight still being impaired I could see nothing. This don't make since! I thought to myself. Why would Davon leave me! My thoughts were interrupted by the groans of the man bleeding like a dog beside me.

"Day!" The groan became louder. "Day, bay is that you, are you here?" "Mmm hmm." "Oh nooo he shot you!" "Yeahhhhh" Davon's tone was a whisper. "Stacie go wit dude let him help you with the kids." "Tell em man up." I was so confused and full of pain. His voice still in a low tone, but I know I heard him right. "Davon please........ hold on baby we need you!" My voice was also low but he heard every word I said thus far. When I received no response I panicked. "Day, Day, c'mon Day don't do this to meeee!" Davon's body was within arms reach. Seeing was impossible so I had to feel around the floor. Davon's body was so close but so far away. My hand rubbed across what felt like a phone.

Thankfully it was the phone. I pressed around on the key pad and found the emergency button. It was Davon's phone but I knew his phone just like it was my own. I hit the button and the phone rung. "911 what is your emergency?" I been ra-ra raped and my boyfriend was shot. I was able to stay on the phone until the dispatcher had all the information he needed, then I collapsed.

The next thing that was partially clear to me was my body rolling down the hallway with bright lights in my face. I could hear Davon's voice in my head. It was like my mind was in one place but my

The doctor tried to explain to me about the surgery that they had to perform, but I was too out of it. Kalief tore my precious jewels to shreds. They took me into surgery right away. It was so brutally ruptured they basically had to construct me a new one. After the surgery I was heavily medicated.

I felt a lot better long as the pain meds were on high volume. My eyes were a different story. I could barely open them, but when I did I rather they stayed closed. They were so sensitive to the light. "Knock Knock." My hospital room door opened. Two detectives came in. The detectives confirmed what I already knew. Davon was dead! He took a bullet to his upper torso. A day had passed and I laid there in the dark with machines and monitors connected to me. For all it was worth I wanted to die. Bringing a baby into this cruel world made me think twice. Because of the brutality of the case I was guarded with a police officer outside of my room.

The officer came in my room and asked me if I knew Awndre Cooper. "Yes Sir." I replied. "Are you up for visitors, he's out there in the hallway." "He can come in." Damn, news travel fast. I thought. But then again what news, because far as I was concerned no one knew. The doctor asked me if I wanted them to call anyone but I could not think of anyone's number off the top. When Dre walked in he said nothing. That made me feel very uncomfortable. "Dre are you there?" Before I heard him speak I got piece of the sniffles. "You better have a cold Dre, I am going to be okay!" "Are you Stacie, and what did they say about the baby, please tell me you two will be okay?" "Stacie what happened to you?" Dre said, not letting me answer the first question. "I was beaten and raped by a person that Davon thought was his friend." "Where was Davon when this happened?" "I don't know where he was at first but now all I know is that he's dead!" I bust out crying. "Huh!" Dre said rubbing my hands. "Yup he walked in on it and he was killed." "Stacie I'm sorry to hear that. I can't imagine what you are feeling right now but I am here for you if you want to talk." Thank you Dre." "So how is the for a while. He made calls to Shalese, Mama, and even tried to reach Tionna for me.

My mama, my mama, I loved her so much! She was beyond devastated. She cried in Dre's ear for about twenty minutes. Dre had to leave the room and then come back. She told Dre she was on her way. I honestly didn't feel like more company but mama wasn't hearing that. She screamed in Dre's ear, "On my way!" Shalese also got real emotional over the phone and for Tionna she was M. I. A. I knew mama and Shalese wanted to come up to see me but I was being released the next day. I didn't see the since in it. Plus, after everything that had happened I needed some time alone. With everyone around, it was much harder for me to grieve properly. The whole time Dre was there, Davon was on my mind and my insides burned with pain. For a while I laid there in silence not knowing where I was going to go home too. Dre had the same concern but this time he didn't ask anything, he demanded. Of course going back to that apartment was not an option. When I asked Dre about Trina, he said what about her. Dre asked me was I up for a little bit of the story. I agreed to listen.

"Trina never came back, we had sex a few times and that was that! I promise you!" For what it was worth I believed him. "Stacie you are my angel saving me from myself." "Saving you from what Dre?" "Self destruction." He said. Dre stayed for another half an hour before he hit the road. Before he left he told me he was picking me up and taking me to get my things from the apartment tomorrow. When he left I was off to sleep.

The next day I was packed up waiting to be released from the hospital. To my surprise guess who was coming down the hallway with Dre? It was my mother, I wondered when and where did they hook up. When mama saw me she panted back and forth like I wasn't even there. She said she came up yesterday too but I was out cold. She said she didn't stay long because she couldn't stand looking at me like mother, look at my baby, look at that pretty face."

Before mama continued there was a knock at the door and then two gentlemen dressed in suites entered the room. They were two more detectives that was working the case. I answered all the questions to the best of my ability. However when the picture came out with Kalief's face on it I choked up. I mean, I choked up real bad. I turned my head away from the picture. The sight of him made me sick. Mama and Dre both surrounded me with support. It was part of the detectives job to get confirmation from me that it was Kalief who did it. Believe me, they already knew who did it! Even when the streets aren't talking, they're talking. I also let them know I wasn't afraid to testify if I had to. Screw that stop snitching crap! He violated me, he violated my baby and he took Day away. It was a must he pay! Me, Mama, and Dre headed to the apartment to get my things. When I got out of the car, two of my neighbors were standing in the parking lot staring.

When they saw my face they quickly turned away and started whispering. As I headed toward the building they looked at me with a strange look. The look was indescribable, it wasn't one of concern. I quickly learned the reason for there looks. My place was no longer there. It was torched, the door was black and police tape outlined it. I just turned around and walked down the steps. While walking back to Dre's car I noticed Davon's car on the other side of the parking lot. I wept like a baby. Dre wrapped his arms around me and made me feel so safe and secure. All Dre's love in the world couldn't stop me from feeling the emptiness of Davon being gone. Every time I thought of him I could hear him groan. What I remember the most was his last words. "Tell dude to take care of the kids." Did he know the whole time the baby could be Dre's. And what did he mean by kids. Why didn't he ever say anything? I wondered. It was too late for any second guessing or wondering. For a quick moment I imagined hugging Davon once more.

depend on a guy to survive. Dre could up and leave me then what! Big-ups to mama she was doing her thing. Later on that day the detectives called me and suggested I go in protected custody. He told me the fire in the apartment wasn't an accident.

The detectives believed it was Kalief or an accomplice. The police department put out a warrant for Kalief's arrest. Soon after he was ghost. The bastard was nowhere to be found. Mama regretted having to leave me, but she had to do what she had to do. It was strange that Tionna never called back, actually she didn't call at all. In the short time we've known each other we got into a lot of crazy stuff together. The game was a regular part of our day. Cooking and bagging coke, counting money, and setting up deals. Besides our money we weren't out to get anybody. It was all about the paper chase. Tionna was in the game doing her thing way longer than I was.

That evening at Dre's crib we caught the local news. There it was after two days and it still made the local head lines. "A young woman, six months pregnant was raped and brutally beaten in her apartment. As her 21 year old boyfriend, Davon Witherspoon walked in on the attack he was shot and killed." Then they showed a picture of Davon's face. The news went on to say the suspect in question was Kalief Howell, and there was a warrant for his arrest. "The suspect is still at large and considered to be armed and dangerous. "I sat there with the remote in my hands feeling numb. Dre was a good man he was there waiting on me hand and foot I loved it, but then I hated it! "Aaaaaaaaaaaaahhh!" I screamed! I couldn't take it no more! I fell to the floor and just screamed. I sat there rocking back and forth.

I hated my life! The pain I was in, the excruciating pain I was in, felt like it was killing me slowly. I've heard the saying, tare you a new butthole, but I didn't think it could really happen. That was never a thought in my mind. Dre just stood there giving me space to get it all out. He said it over and over, let it out, let it out.

but at the projects I built a little rep that I didn't give a damn about anymore. When I finally went back to school it was different, at that moment everyone seemed to care. They threw me a pity party. All of a sudden everybody liked me. I heard the same pity pat crap all day. "Are you okay?" "Do you need anything, I am sorry about what happen to you." Even my teachers were upset behind what happened to me. The teacher who helped me take the exam she felt so bad, she asked me can she be the baby's godmother. Hell yeah I thought to myself! I didn't want to be a victim of her pity party, I said yes though. It might look a little funny but who cares. I wanted the best life possible for my baby and I was going to need help doing it. I received the results of the exam and your girl passed. I then was promoted to the eleventh grade. I was seven months into my pregnancy and school wasn't my favorite place at that time. I liked the bed better. Mama was still hell bent on getting me transferred to the pregnant school. She was due to come home in a week. I was looking forward to it. She deserved to be happy. I know now that her habit was a nasty illness.

It wasn't an excuse but it was fact. Me, I was doing a lot better. My pain had diminished and a sister was horny. I felt bad being horny though. Unfortunately my horny tail needs had to wait. My butt got so big, that sex was very uncomfortable. Even the quickie position, laying on my side wasn't happening. In the meanwhile I was going through hell and Tionna was on the run, because she was scared as hell. When I spoke to Tionna's mom she told me that Tionna left because she was afraid that Kalief would come after her next. Her mom wouldn't tell me where she went, she just said she's out of town. Word on the streets was kind of hard for me to believe. A source told Dre and I that the gang Kalief was rolling with had him tied up in an abandoned basement making him suffer. The source also said that they were upset at the way he handled his business. For all I know that was a crock pot full of bull! I just wanted justice to be served.

found the body they weren't lifting the warrant. Everybody had heard the story about what was suppose to happened to him, but the police wasn't buying it and neither was I. For a while I suffered with having nightmares and post traumatic stress. I can't lie, I hoped in my heart Kalief was dead. Honestly, just having that thought in mind, made me feel a lot better. But then there was Dre, I definitely couldn't bare my drama coming in his life messing anything up.

Between my drama and the countless shit between Dre and Trina we had enough to deal with. If it wasn't for Dre telling her behind off in front of me, I would not have believed him. This trick was a thong! Always in my mans butt! I wore thongs to be sexy but that whore was far from sexy. I mean, she wasn't ugly, but sexy was the wrong word to describe that stank hoe. She was a little rough around the edges and her hair always looked like she just woke up. She could not accept the fact that I was having Dre's baby. Dre told me for years they tried to have a baby and it didn't happen. So I can see why she was so pissed. Trina and I never saw each other face to face. It was when she would pop up and be in the parking lot acting like an ugly fool, that I would see her.

For the next four days Dre was off and a lot had to be done. He surprised me when he told me it was time for me to get my license and he would pay for it. Dre was so busy trying to please me at times, he and I forgot about his own needs. It wasn't intentional but the pregnancy had me drained. It was Tuesday and since I knew he had the next few days off I decided to spice things up. Nothing big, just a little four play. I ran his bath water and put the grown up bubbles in his water. Baking in the oven was two of the finest sirloin steaks. Fresh steamed broccoli and baked mac and cheese. I enjoyed his company that night and the look on his face was priceless. We began the night with soft music and we kissed about a thousand times.

Dre wasn't the type to pressure me into having sex, normally he would just go with the flow. Ultimately, because of the sexual passionate and tender. I had the bedroom chair heated up for him to sit. Leading him to the chair I switched my pregnant behind in front of him giving him a tease. By the time he was in the sitting position his manhood was bulging through his pants. I played around a little bit and my now size ten booty sent chills down his spine. By the expression on his face he looked like he was about to explode. When I turned back around the dude had dropped his pants. It had been a real challenge for me trying to do the oral thing.

Being pregnant had its perks and it sure did have a down side. There was a lot I wanted to do to Dre but after my encounter with Kalief I hesitated. I tried several times but all I would do is gag. That night something had to give. I gave it another shot and to my surprise he enjoyed it. Me personally I didn't think I did anything fancy. Pregnant and all I was able to complete the job. Usually before he could even say babe I'm about to, I would back off real quick! That wasn't the case at all that night. I think I was afraid of the unknown so I had something to prove. Our body's intertwined in a magical moment. Something that was well needed for both of us. The feeling of his juices quenching my every thirst gave me quite a rush. I insisted he make love to me slowly. As usual he was slow but with great aggression. The love making Dre and I shared was always great. Hidden Resentment, Bolding Page/ 142

All though Dre and I had a past before Davon, I still felt guilty. I was suffering from interrupting memories of Davon. Especially the final memories, the night of his death. I managed to block it out for the moment and experience a gigantic orgasm. "Oh My Goodness!" I screamed. As I released myself all over Dre's shaft I shook uncontrollably. The orgasm gave me tremendous pleasure but it felt like another way of crying in some ways. For one, the relief I received was immaculate. But once it was over my emotions were much stronger, everything seemed to be so surreal to me.

Chapter Twelve

Waited around for my little one to arrive. Not knowing the sex was a bit exciting. It was May and I only had one more month to go before I was free of the heavy load. Names were still the furthest thing from my mind. With Trina and her ghetto ass getting on my nerves, I couldn't wait to have my baby. My intentions were not to make it a priority to step to her, but believe me when I say, I want to check her life! The broad never got the message, it was spoken, written, and cursed, at her. If you ask me I think she was a little slow.

One night Dre and I had just went to bed and the door rattled. It was the one and only Ms. Ghetto Fabulous herself. She was standing in the hallway beating the screws out of the door. Before Dre could react I got my big butt up and started wobbling. "Boom, Boom, Boom!" I didn't reach the door before Dre's voice did. I already had a good idea it was her. "Who is it?" Dre yelled. When she said her name Dre jumped up so damn fast, he damn near fell. I swung the door open.

"Yes! Is there something weeeee can help you with?" When I said we I pointed to Dre and then to my belly. The winch turned into a bull with smoke coming from her nose. She stared at my stomach for a quick second then turned to Dre.

"Dre can we talk in private please?" She said trying to sound sexy. By then I was truly sick of her crap! I stood there with my arms about, and further more if you got something to say, say dat shit right here!" I was yawning, and Dre was standing there looking ten karat stupid. "Uuhh somebody betta say sum-thing or this door is bouta shut!" I said, mad as hell. Really, Dre knew that wasn't my steelo so he stepped his game up. "Look Trina I don told you, me and Stacie are together, we are having a baby and that's, that! Now stop coming to my dam house! Bye, and do not come back!" "With that being said, conversation ova!" I said, as I slammed the door in her face. "But Dre I'm pregnant!" She yelled. If I said that whore didn't make me sick I'd be lying. Dre had to get up for work and Mama's graduation was also in the morning. So off to sleep we went. It wasn't no sitting up talking about what had happened. Hopefully she get the picture, that it was over.

I was awakened by a soft and gentle kiss on the lips. "Baby I am leaving, if you need me call me. Please don't forget, if you go in labor don't try to drive." "Haha Dre very funny!" "Sike, but for real call dispatch. It be just my luck I get the call." "Aight baby love you." "Aright babe love you too!" Dre said. It was funny how telling Dre I loved him came so natural but with Davon it was different.

Dre was my first love! This time I wasn't letting that man go anywhere without a fight, and I meant that with my whole heart. It was Lisa's big day, she took her GED test and passed it. The program was hosting a graduation for those who passed. Mama had on all white, she looked like an angel. All the devilish shit she had done, but that day in my eyes she looked like a real life angel. She had been clean for about five months and she was more radiant than ever. As I stood there waiting for her to come down, I had the feelings of a proud parent. After the graduation me and mama went out shopping for house hold goods for her apartment. The program also put her in a one bedroom apartment. Something with just enough space for

The whole time we were out, I was having cramp like pains. I prayed the whole time too! I wasn't trying to go into labor with mama

Gratefully I made home without incident. Back at home laying in the bed my stomach felt like tied rope knots. With every sharp pain my breath was almost taken. Dre finally came in from work and I was still bald up. "Baby! Stacie what's wrong?" "Dre I think it might be time!" I said with agony in my voice. "C'mon baby get yourself together I'm getting you outta here!" "No, baby not yet. I am tryna wait til I know for sure." "And how da hell will we know! We aint never had no baby, you trippin girl!" "It's my dam body and I said not yet, now leave me ALOONE!" The pain hit me harder!

I think Dre was right. He mentioned the other day how the baby had me grouchy, and my response to that was, "Go jerk off!" My hormones were in a rage. I couldn't wait to have that damn baby. I looked like a fat elephant. From a nice size four to a humongous ass 12! That was just ridiculous. If having babies did that to you I didn't want anymore. One was enough anyway! Dre eventually let up and went to take a shower. I was in so much pain and I didn't know why I insisted on being so stubborn. I didn't do dinner or nothing, I just laid there. Dre left his phone on the bed and check this, I decided to be nosy. Now that's some unheard of stuff, I know! I don't know why I started looking at the phone, I thought I trusted him. They, say when you look you shall find. Yeah whatever! In that instance, even if I didn't look I would have found it. The phone started vibrating. The timing couldn't have been more perfect.

"Hello." I said answering. "Oh so now you answering his phone too!" Trina yelled in my ear. "Look trick what do you want you nuisance ass broad!" Dre done told you more than once and you still aint listening! What?" I screamed. "Hmm, I guess I did call at the right time, you sound a bit stressed!" " Bitch never that, how about blessed! Oh right Trina you don't know how labor feel!" "I just wanted Dre to know me being pregnant was a joke! But what I am about to tell your stank ass is not! Tell Dre I had a positive syphilis test, now get that shit checked you home wreckin hoe!" Click up!

Once there I laid his ass out! He didn't even see it coming. "And you say you love me...for real!" I shouted "Syphilis Dre! Get the hell out the shower and take me to the hospital!" Dre didn't get a darn word that was coming out of my mouth. "Stacie what choo just say?" "You heard me I didn't freakin stutter! I tell you what, you and your lil whore Trina betta hope and pray my baby is okay!" Dre hopped out the shower and quickly got dressed. "Stacie what are you talking about?" "How about you call your little whore back and ask her! After this I am done with you and your hoe, I am so sick of these games! Just take me to the hospital to get me and my baby checked!" Once Dre was dressed he picked up his car keys and phone and we headed to the car. I was pissed! I was there, and beyond heated. It was one thing to mess with me but my child, I don't think so!

I endured enough pain, I knew that protecting my baby was my job! Dre got in the car and the tears were steady coming down my face. He was torn and I could tell. But the garbage I had just heard, made me care less about his feelings. There my mind went, I started analyzing everything all over again. Times like that I felt like I needed someone to talk to. I felt like I was about to snap. I had so many mixed, bottled up feelings inside. I felt like a coke a cola bottle about to explode. That Trina trick didn't no who she was messing with. Truthfully the anger I felt scared me at times.

Dre sat there trying to call Trina back. It kept going straight to her voicemail. I was so mad I wasn't telling him anything! One thing I did repeat was, "Syphilis Dre, really!" Is that what she said Stacie?" "I know one darn thing it better not be what my doctor say!" I said. "Dat hoe!" Dre shouted. He beat the stirring wheel and started blurting out all type of stuff. What I didn't understand was how did this girl had so much power over this man. We were about five minutes away from the hospital when my panties and sweat pants filled with hot wet liquid. For a second the dumbest thing ran across my mind. I know this chick don't have me that upset that I'm sitting here pissing on myself. I had to remember I was pregnant. Then it instantly dawned on me that it was my water breaking.

room lot the pain was damn near unbearable. "Call mama Dre." Although Trina just laid a heavy stick on me I still needed him. Several doctors came to my aid to prepare me for delivery. It was so embarrassing to have to tell the doctors about the syphilis scare, but it had to be done. Because I initially changed clinics during my prenatal care he had to request my records from the first clinic. To take the precaution measures the doctor injected some medication through a needle into my butt. What was suppose to be the most happiest time of my life; I was immortally crazed.

The baby was doing his thing getting ready for his entrance into the world. Dre tried to cheer me up until the anesthesiologist came but it wasn't working. I wanted him to shut the hell up! "Stacie have you thought of a name yet?" "Yeah a feeeeew!" And there went that conversation. My contractions were about two minutes apart. By the time I was getting myself together from the first one there came another one. Mama ran in the room so happy. If she only knew that I was so sad. "My baby is so pretty!" Mama said. "I love you my Stacie, you doing so good." I managed to put on a fake smile.

"AAAAhhhhh............HELP! Ma tell the doctor I gotta poop!" Mama laughed. "Stacie that might be the baby, you might be ready girlfriend!" Dre was a freaking dork, he paced back and forth until mama read his behind! "Awndre if you don't get over here and comfort my daughter you don't wanna know what!" "I'm, I'm, I'm sorry!" Dre stuttered. I just sucked my teeth. Mama butt was so busy fussing at Dre, she never went and got the doctor. Luckily they had monitors at the station. The monitor showed my heart rate drop severely with the last contraction. They came running in. "Ok Ms. McCall we're gonna check you now." The doctor said. Ms. McCall what's your pain from zero to ten." "Are you kidding me it's a hundred! Now get this baby outta Meeeeeeeee!" "Where's da anesth......ane, whateva he is." Come on Stase it's going to be okay." Mama said. The doctor went to do the exam and the baby's head was already crowning. The doctors had no time to prepare anything else.

huh." I replied. My chin was to my chest and I gave all I had pushing. With each push Davon's face flashed in my head. What if this baby is his, what will I do? After the fourth push the doctor made her announcement. "Congratulation you are the parents of a beautiful baby girl." On the inside I was jumping for joy but yet in still, the fear still lingered on. All of a sudden more pain over powered me. It was another contraction! When the doctor went in for the afterbirth she made another startling announcement. "Oh my goodness mom did you know you were having twins? We gotta another baby here!" I thought I had finally gone crazy! This is a joke right, I thought to

For a moment everyone around me was trying to stop me from breaking down. "Stacie no matter what, you know I love you and I'm here for you!" Dre said that loud and clear. "Stacie, God is not going to put more on you than you can handle." Mama said. "Stacie honey you gotta push we don't want the baby to go into distress." That baby was stubborn, instead of four pushes it was nine. I had two little bundles of joy. Mama wanted a piece of naming the twins. We named them Makai and Makaya. Mama loved the name Malikai who was Gods messenger. So I just put a little twist on it. The hours after the birth of my babies turned into really mushy ones. Forgetting everything about my past and focusing on my babies helped a shift in my mood though.

They were so beautiful and full of life. It would be unfair to them for me to be sour, so sad, and angry. Their little lives were just beginning. Mama went to get me something to eat and left Dre and I to talk. The talk was a well needed one. We had some major issues to work out. Not only the Trina mess, but I wanted to get a blood test. Dre tried to convince me not to get the blood test, but I needed to know the truth. On the strength of Davon that wasn't an option. I couldn't just ignore his memory. That part of the past I wanted to put behind me and move on. "Davon!" I shouted. "After Davon was and shook my head.

Dre thought Davon's death was a touchy subject so he rarely said much about it. Dre never commented, he looked at me and rubbed my neck. I didn't expect him to say anything but I needed him to know that it was okay to talk about it. What if the babies are Davon's, they also deserve to know the truth one day. I wondered could Dre live with that or would he walk away. The doctor came in to give us an update on the babies. The girl was stubborn not wanting to eat and the boy was eating everything. "Ms. McCall is it okay if we discuss your medical file that we retrieved from the other clinic." I assured him that whatever was in the file Dre should hear it too. "Stacie there were a few test performed on you in your first trimester of pregnancy. The test included HIV, Hepatitis, and a series of STD test. All of your results were recorded negative except for your syphilis test. So you're telling me I have syphilis!" "We'll say had, because that shot we gave you took care of that."

"Technically speaking, you shouldn't have any more problems there. However I am concerned with the length of time you had it, and the babies." "What? What about them?" I said scared. "Can they be affected by this?" "I'm afraid so!" "Syphilis can blind newborns coming through the canal at birth. If it gets in his or her eyes." "You are considered to be lucky, your babies could of been still born. Don't panic Stacie, we'll do everything we can to ensure the health of your babies." The doctor left the room. "You know Dre, since Trina gave that bit of information, I've been confused. Dre I have searched all the possibilities high and low. Knowing that I had syphilis even before my babies were in me give me all the answers I need." "But Stacie!" "NO you're gonna let me finish! I have forgiven you for being such a weak man but I never gave you credit for being a stupid one. You put me and the lives of my babies in harms way, and the way I feel somebody has to pay."

****

who felt like they could wrong me and get away with it would be sorry. Maybe I was the reason people did cruddy hurtful things to me. I was a damn puss for so long! Not any more, I proclaimed! When the doctor read my results Dre looked so dumb. I wanted to smack his ass! I wanted to see if he was man enough to stay and listen to the babies results. Just the thought of the situation made my blood boil!

Even though I had mama to talk too I still had the all alone syndrome. Truthfully, Dre was the last person I wanted to talk too. And mama, oh well, that was a different story. The thing with her was, I didn't want her to have to deal with so much so early. Stress was the last thing she needed. The two people in my life that I loved so dear, I also had hatred toward them at one point. I was so happy to have mama back in my life that I blocked out all the negative shit from the past. Once again something that I had to talk about stayed inside. For the sake of the babies I had to do things right.

In the hospital room I packed me and the twins stuff and then waited on Dre to come. He had already told me he was going to be late because he was going to the clinic to get treated. At that point I could care less. As far as I was concerned his penis could fall off! That's how angry I was. Long as he was there for the babies, I was good. Dre said he was going to stop at Walmart to get the baby a car seat. Neither one of us expected twins. When the doctor came in I was in there alone. That time there were two of them. As soon as I saw them enter the room my heart dropped.

"Good morning Stacie how do you feel?" "I'm okay I guess." I replied. "I see you're all ready to go home with your babies." "Yup!" "Stacie we ran several test on the babies and they seemed to be fine. Because they are so young we can't tell if something is wrong with their sight yet. The damage, if any could show up later.

"One test we did consist of drops in their eyes. Under normal circumstances if their sight was effected the solution wouldn't bother process is reliable. Makai responded to the drops and Makya did not." "What?" "But like I said before that does not mean that she's blind. We will have to give it a little more time." "How much more time?" I said, confused. "It could be anywhere from two to four months." Then the other doctor said, "Stacie don't think the worst, we do not know anything for sure yet." After the doctors left my mood dampened a little but I refused to handle this like a puss yet again. I sucked up my sadness and moved on.

Chapter Thirteen

Mama was a major help. Not only was she an awesome grandma, she kept her word and got me transferred. Even though I had already had the twins the school still accepted me because they were under six months. The pregnant school had different rules and credit requirements than normal public schools. The counselor told me that I only needed two more credits to graduate high school. You know that was music to my ears! Life was starting to go in a good direction for me again. The time that I had out of school I turned my learners permit into a full drivers license. My two credits came like candy, Sweet! Dre and I were still not humping but that was the last thing on my mind. Trina was still a plane butt hole! The popping up stopped but she continued to call. Dre was so naive I had to make the suggestion that he get his number changed. His Daddy skills topped the charts I must say. He was the ultimate father. Deep in my heart I wanted to be with him, I didn't know if I should though. I wondered if I could trust him. I wouldn't label him the cheating type but he was dependent as hell! It's as if he couldn't live without a darn woman!

Each day that went by, Dre did something different to ease back in my good grace and my panties. What he didn't know was I peeped the guy next door and I was feeling him. Yeah, he was a hustler but he was low key with it. We spoke maybe once or twice that's all. I wasn't fitting to make the same dumb mistakes over and over. If I said that I wasn't sexually frustrated then I would be lying. However it became harder and harder. The same saga happened each night. I would get in the bed all oiled down in my boy shorts and bra, with Dre beside me in his boxers and wife beater.

Since I had the babies my baby fat was beautiful. My breast was big and full. My booty was plumper than it had ever been, and a chick stomach was gone. Dre's manhood would get so hard he would have to prop a pillow between his legs. One night he literally had to go in the bathroom to calm down. I got up to get something for the baby and dude was in the bathroom going hard, jerking off! Now that almost got me! Seeing that big chunk of flesh I wanted to give in completely. I wanted to taste him like never before. Horny was I! Instead I giggled and shut the door. As bad as I wanted him, he had to show me something different when it came to Trina. I felt like she got away with too much. In the process of dogging him she hurt me and mine!

Dre should have done something! I mean, I don't know what, but damn do something! Far as the twins, so far so good. Every doctors appointment that the twins went to, went well. The appointment thereafter was no exception. The doctor said that they both looked great. When we Left the doctors appointment, I drove down Eager street. "SCCUUURRR!" I slammed on the breaks. My eyes had to be going bad. It was Kalief! "Oh babies I'm so sorry.......mommy sorry!" I comforted the twins before driving off. That bastard wasn't dead! It was all a lie! When I saw him, I slammed on breaks. Not thinking at all about my babies. Not to mention the screeching noise would only bring more attention to my car. Kalief's head turned my way and his eyes mounted to my car. When my eyes met his, I looked in his face and sped off. That bastard was evil! The look on his face reminded me of the jokers face from the movie batman.

I raced home, trying to get my babies safe was the first thing on my agenda. Dre was at work but he had to know exactly what I knew. I decided not to call him at work. He would be worried all day at

That bs we heard about Kalief was a lie Mama! I'm scared Mama!"
"Say what Stacie!" "Yes Mama you heard me!" "He saw us mama,
me and the babies! I am scared Mama, he might come after us!"
"Fuck dat!" Mama said. "You and my babies don't go home, come
here until Dre get off! If that bastard want it he better come correct
this dam time! Stacie we aint gon run from his punk ass, don't he
gotta warrant anyway! Stacie yall just come on!"

"This time we gonna deal with this bastard!" Mama made me feel
a lot tougher than I really was. It was the tone in her voice that was
so reassuring. While me and the babies were over Mamas house we
ate, talked, laughed and played. Mama asked me if I had spoken to
Tionna. I told her that I did not, and as far as I was concerned I was
leaving it alone. Although I was worried about her, she could have
picked up the phone to call as well! What mama said after that made
a whole lot of sense. "Stacie we don't know what this ill bastard got
up his sleeve, so right now you trying to contact Tionna definitely
wouldn't be on no friendship bull! This is more about you and my
grand babies safety."

It was three o'clock when I dialed Dre's phone. "What up Stase?"
Dre joked when he answered his phone. "Baby come past mama's
house when you get off." "Dammm what I do to get called baby?" "I
did just say that didn't I!" I said to myself. "Dre listen, just come to
mama's house okay!" He heard the urgency in my voice and put all
jokes aside. Then he returned the gesture and called me baby. The
babies were with mama a lot during the week, so she had enough
changing clothes and diapers for them at her house. She demanded
the babies stay with her the weekend until me and Dre hash some
things out. Meaning, figure out how we were going to handle this
Kalief chaos. She also thought it was time for him and I to move
on from the past. "Mama I don't know if I can stay away from my
babies for three nights!" "Girl you be aight!" She shouted. Yeah, she
thought the weekend started on Thursday. She wanted them from
Thursday to Sunday.

me smile back. He came close to hug me and I inched back. I heard Lisa nosy behind say, "Stacie!" I rolled my eyes at Dre, but still smiling. I finally leaned in to give him a hug. "Do you know these babies see everything! Stacie you need to move on and forgive him or let him go!" Mama said. "Everybody makes mistakes." "Aright Mama I get it!" Mama was definitely right but the little devil in me said, yeah easy for you to say. After ignoring everything else mama said I turned to talk to Dre.

"Dre mama is keeping the babies this weekend because we have a few things to deal with." "Ms. Lisa you taken my babies!" Dre said to mama. "I know one thing yall better learn how to share them babies with me!" I just looked at her and shook my head. She have them all through the week what more did she want. "Aright now yall get out and go talk!" "Aright Ms. Lisa, Dre said kissing the babies goodbye. I led the way home as Dre closely followed behind me. Mama only lived about eight minutes from us.

Dre and I arrived home and like always, before we could talk he had to take his shower. I told him he had a bad case of OCD. He couldn't think straight without taking a shower first. When Dre came out of the shower he came in the room dripping wet. manhood swinging and all. That punk knew exactly what he was doing! I immediately turned my head and put my hand over my face. When I looked up his man was muscled to the max.

I turned my face to the wall like a kid and burst out laughing. He jumped on me hard muscle and all, rubbing it in between my thighs and teasing my every inch. I tried very hard to keep my composure. "I have to keep my composure." I kept telling myself. I couldn't tell my throbbing kitten that, she wanted him and she wanted him right then! My entire body relaxed and Dre felt it. We started kissing and rubbing each other like we just met. The kisses were magnificent. Right when I was about to give in fully my phone rang.

was glad the phone rang because I wasn't finish tormenting him yet! However, in the meantime I was being tormented too. My phone read private call. When I picked it up no one said anything.

"Dre today when I was coming from the clinic I saw Kalief!" "He is not dead baby!" Dre's eyes got buck wide, and his body leaned to the side. "Are you effen kidding me?" He said. Dre got up walked in the kitchen and opened the cabinet over the refrigerator. He wasn't playing at all, the dude pulled out a nine millimeter. "Wow!" I said. After I saw that piece I was speechless. Damn I guess I was the only scared one. "Stacie this is the safety lock, this is the trigger, this is........" "Hold up, hold up, hold up! Dre, What the hell man! Do you really expect me to use this?" "Hell yeah if you have too!" He was right so I took the lesson and closed my mouth. He showed me everything from locking it to reloading it.

After he was done, I had crazy respect for the black beauty. "Dre I know you don't expect me to carry this thang around do you?" "Yup, and if he gets to close you better use it too! Oh, and if you have to use it, make sure you kill em!" At that gesture we both laughed. "Dre there is something else we have to talk about. Dre the babies are three months and as much as you're against the blood test we need to have one done." For a long minute Dre didn't say a word. "Okay set up the appointment and let me know so I can take off." I loved him even more for that. His giving and his respectfulness always turned me on. "Oh yeah, one more thing boo. What do you think about us moving. The kids really need there own room. I am sure you can agree it's getting pretty tight in here. Plus I am going back to work in two more weeks so you do not have to do things by yourself." "Going back to work where?" Dre joked. Jumping on top of him I said, the hair salon silly!

"Don't say another word!" I demanded. I tongued him down like he was my favorite ice cream. He eased off my leggings and shirt, then commenced to playing in my pudding bowl. Hearing the wet enjoyed each other. "Dam girl I love the hell out a you!" "Prove it Dre!" I moaned. Between the moaning and panting I could barely catch my breath. Dre then turned me over and laid me flat on my

Dre caressed my back and butt with his penis. The tickling sensation felt so good. At that point I wasn't ashamed to admit he had all of my heart and soul. He used my favorite body oil, with his penis still in position he poured the oil down the small of my back. He grabbed both of my plump round cheeks and put every bit of himself in my world. I nearly screamed! I was taken aback by the pleasurable penetrating feeling. It was the force of nature that brought us together. That moment was going down in my history book as a moment of passion, pain, and adult only pleasure. We humped for hours, switching positions and experiencing each others moisture all over the apartment.

The next morning Dre got up for work, at least that's what I thought. He wanted to suck up the opportunity to spend as much quality time with me. So when he got up to go in the bathroom he called out from work. "Good morning baby!" Dre said. "Hey you!" I replied. Dre came over to give me a kiss and I hurried and put the pillow over my face. "No Dre my breath stink! Move Boy!" "Girl give me a kiss! I smelled your funky breath before!" I frowned my face and gave him a kiss. "C'mon get dressed." "Where are we going Dre?" "Just get dressed and you will see." He is too darn smart, I thought! "And Stacie put something comfortable on, no heels!" "Uh huh! Who in the hell do he think he is! First he don't wanna tell me where we are going, and now he telling me how to dress." I mumbled to myself. We ate breakfast then we hit the town. The weather was marvelous. It was mid September and it was probably around 80 degrees or so. Columbia mall was our first stop.

Once we arrived at the mall we ate brunch. Personally I wasn't hungry but Dre was a different story. This was something that Dre way. This guy was really proving himself. Before he came into my life I was practically Steeling or borrowing everything I had. I never imagined I would ever be able to afford anything from Bakers. I looked at Dre with the goofiest look on my face. I put my hand over my mouth like we had just won the lottery. "Get what you want." He said. I wasn't a picky chick but I learned to be more tasteful hanging with Shalese and Lisa. I dared not to pick something too expensive. But I be a dumb ass if I didn't get something worth my wild. I pointed to the Ugg boots.

"Babe are these too much?" I whispered. "Didn't I say get what you want! Wait up, you gon dance for me in them right?" Dre said laughing. "And you know this!" I said smiling. "Get something else too, you can't wear them everyday." I got a pair of tan flat rider boots and a pair of all white shell heads just to make him happy. The total came up to two hundred and seventy nine dollars. I was happy as I don't know what! I figured our day was done until he took me to yet another store. This time he took me to the limited. "Look Dre I know I said prove it but baby money is not want I meant by it!" "Stacie I can't lie and say I'm not trying to get in your good grace because I am. However I know money is not the answer. I learned you along time ago boo, just trust me please!"

"I know you are from a total different breed. I did do a lot of buying love with Trina and I see where that mistake got me. I don't mean to mention her name but it's the truth." "Plus your fat ass need some clothes! I'm tired of seeing you in stretch pants and sweats." "Aright Dre watch your mouth!" "Naw I'm for real! I know you can't fit your old clothes, so why don't you start fresh and buy all new ones." "You're serious aren't you?" "Yeah, I'm dead serious. We can take your old clothes to the good will or something." "Aw Dre I love you!" We both smiled. "I thought you said money don't buy love! " "Shut up boy I loved you before today! But I don't know Dre, about giving away my old clothes. This body gonna get back into my old clothes one day." Dre proceeded, he hit me on my butt and said, "But

I truly did love my shape, it had took on a shape of womanhood. I definitely felt more like a woman than a little girl. After about three hours of shopping I was tired. Dre had the balls to ask me if I was hungry again. That man was crazy! I didn't know if he was serious or not. When I declined yet another meal he suggested we go talk. He was on some ole unusual stuff that day! I was usually the big talker. Sitting at the bar, Dre ordered two Ciroc an cranberry juices. "Here let me make a toast." "To what may I ask?" I said enthusiastically. "To better days I guess." He replied.

Mind you, I haven't drank anything since my birthday. "Dre I hope you know, what you are getting yourself into!" We went three more rounds after that. I got up to go to the bathroom and tripped in Dre's lap. "See I told you, you're in good hands." He responded. Instead of going straight to the bathroom we held a miniature conversation. "Stacie you are so beautiful!" "When I look into your eyes I still see so much hurt and pain. For our babies sake I'm asking you to let it go." "I hope you can move past the hurt I've caused you and let's build a foundation for our family." "Dre not right now, today was a perfect day let's talk about something else." "Yes as soon as you give me an answer!" "Dre I'm over it, I love you and that's it!" "Now whether we stay together and happy, the ball is in your court! You have me.... all of me, I promise." "Dat's all a man need ta hear!" Dre said. He done turned me into a vulnerable sucker. With his fine brown self!

Coming from the bathroom I could see Dre looking in his phone and even as I got closer he never put it away. "You know what Stase I been meaning to tell you this." "Oh goodness what Dre!" "I loooooove you guuuurl!" He said, singing it so loud. I was embarrassed as I don't know what! I ran ahead of him to the car. Dre and I put a night cap on things over a few games of madden and some hot wet mushy sex. We checked in with mama and she told us that the kids were fine. She had already put them in the tub and was getting them ready for bed. Mama also warned me not to call back because she was waiting on her sugar daddy.

for Dre and I. Football was back in session so Dre was on the field a lot. I was a day away from going back to the salon. The kids had a follow up appointment and at least two days a week Dre took me to the shooting range.

Knowing Kalief was still alive bugged the hell out of me. Out of the clear blue I finally heard from Tionna. Tionna was a good person to have in your comer because she picked up all the gossip. Difference between her gossip and other peoples was her shit was legit most of the time. When we talked it wasn't for long but she also knew Kalief was alive. The phone was never a good way to do business in the hood so the conversation was quick as possible. Dre was my baby he took real good care of me and the twins.

I was doing my thing at the salon, even on a bad day I would still come home with at least two fifty in my pocket. A sister wasn't complaining. Today was the big day. The day that we begin on the road of truth and get the dna done. On the way to the lab to get the test done Dre was still trying to get me to change my mind. I think he was honestly afraid that the babies were going to be Davon's, While we waited to go in the back the lab technician handed Dre some paper work to fill out. Thank God for modern technology we did not have to get stuck by any needles. The swabbing of the mouth

Dre and I both had been tired from the long hours we had put in at work. Not to mention the twins and there non sleeping schedule. "Home sweet home!" Kya always laughed when I said that. The babies were six months, and they were bad as hell but they brought so much joy to our lives. "Babe I be back Ima go and get the mail" "Hurry up Dre, don't be tryna get out of helping me undress them!" I said with a smirk on my face. "Haha you got jokes....You know I do anything for my seeds." "Okay there not seeds anymore Dre, they are babies. What happens Dre if the babies aren't yours, we never discussed that part?" "They are mine!" Dre said, then he walked out of the door. That was my hint to shut up, point blank period.

up like we hadn't checked it for days. Looking through the pile, there was a letter from EBMC that stood out. That had to be opened immediately. C'mon Stase open the mail tomorrow, let me put you to sleep while the babies are sleep." "As much as I love the way you are thinking this letter can't wait." "How you sound anyway, if you didn't want me to open the mail why did you get it. Boy you crazy." "What is it Stacie?" "It's the letter about the babies." "Oh aight!" "To the parent or guardian of Makya Cooper. The recent test results indicate limited if any eye sight in her left eye. It is imperative that she is seen immediately. We also have reason to believe her eye could still be infected as well."

"Please don't further delay this matter, call to schedule an appointment as soon as possible." The look on my face spoke a million words. "Tell me it's not bad news babe!" "I'm Done." I replied in the most calmest voice. "What it say?" My freakin baby is blind all because yo nasty tail and your whore!" "Stop playing, let me see!" "Are you serious Dre, do you really think I would lie about something like this!" My voice began to elevate. "Dre I told you once before, Trina had to be dealt with and you wanted me to forgive all! I was cool with that at first, now screw dat! You didn't wanna hear nothing I had to say and now my baby is paying the consequences for this bull!" Not letting Dre say anything I just kept going. "I left this mess in your hands way too long! Oh you betta believe she won't get away with hurting my baby!"

There Dre sat looking dumb founded, again! "So what are we gonna do Dre?" I said whispering but nasty." "What the heck do you want me to do Stacie?" Dre snapped. "It was me okay, I should of known dam better! Yeah I knew she was a hoe and I still continued to sleep with her! Blame me okay!" "You know what Dre to hell with you! You know what, I do blame your weak ass, won't you go handle dat trick!" "Either way it's me or her and that's real talk!" "To hell with me Stacie, dat's how you feel.......eff me, Okay!" "Look at choo Dre flipping shit so it can benefit you, when it come to my kids you and with you, eff you or whateva, AND!" Dre left out and slammed the door behind him.

Kya woke up screaming. "C'mon baby it's gonna be okay." I rocked her and started crying myself. "God not her too....She don't deserve a hard life to start. Please God help my baby!" There was something in Kya's eyes that I never saw before then. My baby had a sparkle that looked as if she had a glass eye. I cried harder just looking at her. I started shaking and panicking. I really started to lose it. Kaya was back to sleep, then it all came to me. I had a plan. Trina messed with the wrong one. Everything that she said started playing back in my head. "Me pregnant that shit is a joke, Tell em I tested positive for syphilis. Now check dat out!" I put my face into the pillow and screamed.

Once I reflected on my plan once more I calmed down. Just knowing she had an ass whooping coming, I was cool. "You have reached the voicemail box of........Dre! Please leave your message after the beep." I pray I didn't push Dre to far, far enough to go looking for her. I wanted that girl all for myself. I'm not a lesbian but I wanted Trina's entire body. I called Dre back. "Hello." "Dre come home we need too talk. Dre was actually crying! "Stacie I am so sorry, I'm soo sorry! But you're right, Ima find her ass and I'm gonna stomp a mud hole in dat ass!" "NO! Dre listen to me sweetie come home so we can talk, I promise we will be okay just come home!" When Dre came home I let him in on the little bit I had in mind to convict Trina. "Dre Trina will get hers but it has to be from woman to woman, so will you help me?"

"Yeah anything you want." "Aright let's get one issue behind us first, the blood test. Then I'll be happy to move forward. I will call the clinic in the morning to see if we can get an appointment for her tomorrow evening. Will you be able to make it." "No doubt, I will get off early." "Okay I'll cancel my appointments at the salon and I'll call you to tell you what time the appointment is set for." Trying

Woooo, that dream felt too real! In my dream I beat the cowboy shit out of her! Whooping Trina's behind was something that I wanted to do. I never considered myself violent, and I also knew it wouldn't fix Kya's eyes, but I would enjoy the pain that she would have to

Chapter Fourteen

The whole story about Kalief was obviously a crock of crap! Did he want revenge, was he on the run? For the last few months I have been his point of interest. Without making himself known he was silently tracking me. He blamed me for everything that went wrong in his pathetic life. What he failed to realize was that the messy life he had, did not start with me. By any means necessary he wanted to pay me back.

Now Trina, let's talk about that chick! She was the biggest freak hoe, she liked sucking everything, on everyone and didn't mind a few twinkies for doing it. The whore ran through Baltimore with open legs and arms! The fact that Kalief bumped into her wasn't know damn accident. That was all apart of his plan. Tracking me, he found her and her weakness. Trina was so naive. Kalief told her that I was his ex, and since Dre was her ex they should make our lives miserable. When the devil lurk, he stops at nothing! She fell for every part of it. There was no doubt how much Trina really loved Dre, it was just too late for her to prove it. When she had him she didn't know what to do with him. Him being able to move on was something she couldn't stomach. All the while Kalief's plan didn't only involve hurting hearts.

He wanted me dead and was willing to go as far as killing Dre to do it. Me seeing him couldn't have been a mistake on his part. He wanted me to see his low life behind. He thought it would scare the

I was looking forward to revenge being all mine. Whether it was Kalief or Trina calling my phone it didn't even matter anymore, because surely the tables was about to turn. I had to get into his head. What type of sick piece of shit was he? Remembering what he did to me, I knew he was not satisfied that I was alive and well. He wanted me to suffer, but this time I plan to call the shots. If I had to suffer it was going to be my way.

So much of my young life was left up to the way other people played their cards. For once it was going to be about what I said! In the past weeks I've done a little research myself. I learned that Trina and Kalief were together a lot. And Oh, I also found out I wasn't Kalief's only target. I was just the biggest. Kalief resented me, for what, I don't know! I never took Davon away from him. Far as Trina, she hated my guts because I was fly as hell, younger than her, and her ex impregnated me with twins! At least I hope so. I tell you what, even if that wasn't the case that hoe would never know. Before now I didn't have anything to fight for. Huh... now my kids was all the reason I need!

Before those beauties came in my life I could care less if I died or not. Today all I think about is living, and I mean living good too! At first I didn't know what I wanted for Dre and I. Then it hit me, if all Dre turned out to be was a good father to the kids, then I would be grateful for that. I had already dealt with a fair share of hurt and pain, and there was no man alive that could come and erase that. We are all human and we all screw up. However when the same person get screwed over to many times, you better pray and hope it's not you who done it for the last time.

Chapter Fifteen

Dre was at work and the mail was in my hands. I sat there Contemplating whether I should wait until he got home to open it. There were two letters from the lab. I found that to be so stupid. We told them we live together but it was still their policy to mail each person involved in the test a copy of the results. What if the babies were Davon's, I thought. I don't know if I can handle the look on Dre's face if they are. It was a must I found out right then. I had to prepare myself for the big what if.

Without further hesitation I ripped open the envelope. Reading.......... reading and reading. "What the hell do all these numbers mean? Huh, this can't be right!" Now I am pacing back and fourth because the results are unbelievable. "Do this say what I think it says?" I questioned myself. "No way this can't be right! " The results were not what I expected. To be honest I didn't even know that this madness was possible! The results were so shocking and my emotions were confused. Crying wasn't an option, laughing was more of how I felt. Laughing would have been just plain wrong because that was not a laughing matter at all. On that note I had to call Lisa!

"Ma guess what!" "What?" Mama said, all stupid! "Ma stop playing, the DNA test results are back!" "Ooooh did they! Well what the results say dammit?" Mama I got two baby daddys and I only been pregnant once! Mama I'm a hoe!" Mama laughed her butt off. "Girl you sure you reading that thang right?" "Yeah, I think so! Beside girl, is there a number on it so you can call?" "Yeah it is." "Listen Stacie I think we should know for sure before you share this with Dre." "I feel you Mama but truthfully if this is correct he won't find out anyway." "And how you suppose to do that Stacie?" "Mama I'll forge some crap if I have to!" "Oh Lord, call them and call me back."

I think at times she felt guilty about not being there. So instead of being my mother she accepted the friendship role. She could have also been afraid that I would have rejected her as my mother. Which in all actuality it makes perfect since. She wasn't there so how could she come in my life now that I am grown and call any shots. The tone in her voice let me know she wasn't happy about what I was planning to do but she never said anything. For so long mama and I were not on the same page, it felt good to finally be on the same accord. The lady at the lab confirmed what I thought. One baby was Dre's and the other baby was Davon's. That result by far was the craziest mess I had ever heard, or read for that matter!

It was the bizarre truth that Dre could never find out! So I made up my mind that until I went and got the papers altered, that he wouldn't know anything. The babies appointment was in two days so I needed them before or by then. My goal was to get it done and have them by the next day. It was a computer and printer at the salon so the forgery wouldn't be impossible. I'll take both letters with me and do me.

Interrupting my thoughts, my phone rang. It was the private caller again. "All this time I had this phone and now all of a sudden someone wants to play on it." When the private number called most of the time I would send it straight to my voicemail. Sometimes I would get the urge to answer it, and when I did it would be some butthole breathing in my ear! The next day at work I was tickled pink. I have to admit, I was having a good day. I still could not believe the truth though. A set of twins that have different fathers. They came from the same womb at the same damn time. "What in the hell was this in three hours. I was so anxious and I could barely wait to get off.

When my last customer was done I went and did the magic. After I was done I held the paper up to the light and it looked good and real to me. They say everything come to the light. So what a good way to bring it to the light, where only I could see it! I laughed out loud at that one myself. That night had to be extra special, I wanted to bring nothing but good news for a change to Dre. For the love of my kids I would do any damn thing! I could of felt bad but I didn't! The results were just for my personal knowledge anyway. Dre never wanted the truth.

They deserve to have him as their father. I couldn't see my children's life start rough or without a fighting chance. Unlike me, they would have options and a damn good father! I left the twins at mama's after work and went straight home. I had a few things that I had to do, like go get dinner and diapers. Plus I wanted to get started on dinner before I got the little rascals. Dre agreed to pick them up after his football practice. It wasn't a good idea to have two six month old babies out in the brisk weather while I ran errands. Mama was cool with that, because anytime with her grand babies was special.

Shalese was a trip these days. She came by the shop today and I did her hair. I told her that Dre turned out to be the father and she was glad. I wasn't about to tell everybody my damn business. Mama knew not to run her mouth too. Ultimately she still found it funny too. Shalese and her dad were really coming to a head. She text me on the way to the market about what he said smart about her hair. Once I got in the market I texted her back. In the market I could not decide what to make for dinner. Dre was a seafood man, and that night it was about pleasing him. I picked up some crab meat, corn on the cob, shrimp and tossed salad. I sped home so I could get a good head start on things before Dre got there with the children. I was able to cook and shower before my family came home. After I got out of the shower I heard the apartment door close. Perfect timing

Hidden Resentment

I thought. "Dreeeee!" "Yeah babe!" "Yaaaay my favorite people are home!" I said enthusiastically. "Look on the table babe!" "Oh shux this is the results!" "Yup!" "Why you didn't open em!"

"Wait Dre don't open them yet, let's do it together!" "Hurry up boo!" "Good things come to those who wait!" I said jokingly. "Hello family." I kissed Dre and the kids hello. "Aww look at my babies, it's cold out dare! Mommy know! I love yall, and look at you Kya, what grandma do to your hair? I liiike!" After the babies were undressed

"The hour has come, shall I, or do you want to do the honors?" Dre told me to do it, then he had the nerve to say, "Cause you're the one who wanted to know." "Are you being sarcastic Dre?" "No, but I'm scared as hell though!" "Alright I'll do it give me a drum roll." Dre beat both his hands on the table and Kya burst out laughing. She was so goofy. I took my sweet time opening the envelope. "C'mon Stase look at the results!" He said. Then I pretended to get anxious like I

"Okay hole-up I see a lot of numbers." "Give me Stase, because you playing!" Dre snatched the damn paper! "Whoop, Whoop!" Dre yelled. He looked like a dag on fool dancing around the house. I covered my mouth with my hands seeing his reaction. I knew he saw that he was the daddy. He ran over to me and swept me off my feet. We kissed hard and rough like some fools on a movie. We then realized the twins were looking at us like we were the fools. If they only knew. With a melody playing in his soul he was able to take care of his stinking hygiene. Which was so unusual for him. Normally his shower came first. He literally could not do anything without a shower. Hidden Resentment, Bolding Page/ 179

"Mmmm baby what's that you cooking, it smell good!" "Oh I thought you were talking about me, but it's your favorite." "I fixed some crab cakes among other things." "I knew you loved me!" "There you go Dre, don't start with me! You know I love you!" "I know you do." Dre and I ate dinner and were stuffed. What we thought was going to turn into a romantic evening turned into a crying fest. Good thing Dre took off the next day for Kya's appointment because they cried until two in the morning. We didn't know what the hell was wrong with them! Then Dre decided to call mama. We were her means of income, so we knew she did not have to get up and go to work because the kids wouldn't be there in the morning. That was a bright idea I told Dre.

Mama shocked the hell out of me because she really knew a little something. Not to mention she only had one child of her own. Mama told us that the twins were teething. Dre ran to seven eleven to get some Motrin and Orajel. After a good dose of medicine they were done! Having sex was the last thing on our mind after that. Gratefully the appointment was after eleven in the morning. Dre held me tighter than ever before. "Dre I don't know if I can handle tomorrow!" "The appointment!" "Yeah, Dre please don't renege on me, I really want the opportunity to talk to Trina woman to woman. I know it might not make any sense to you, but I have to get this off of my chest. I promise it won't get ugly but it's something I have to do." "I said I would, so I will." I was overly excited to confront her face to face and not be pregnant. To be honest, even I didn't know what I was looking to gain from it.

I hoped Dre was not just saying that to shut me up. Dre had no clue about Trina and Kalief collaborating and that's how I planned on keeping it. But I be darn if I allow any one of those psychos to catch us off guard!

*****

I had butterflies in my stomach, it was appointment time. The appointment couldn't go any slower. The twins were getting cranky and tired of sitting still. They were at that age where they wanted to explore the floor and put everything in their little mouths. "Makya Cooper." Finally I thought. The medical assistant called Kya's name. "Hello mom is this dad?" "Yes." I replied. "How are we doing today?" "We could be better." Dre said. "Did anyone explain to you what is going on with Makya's eye sight?" "We got a letter that's about it." "In Makya's left eye there is limited or no sight. In her right eye it indicate strain and muscle tension which also indicate it could be affected." Tears formed in my eyes and I tried my best to hold them back. It hurt like hell to know my innocent baby was going through that already. Let alone she was my baby!

I could hear Dre asking the doctor questions and her answering him. To say I heard what was said I would be lying. All I could think about was punching Trina in her ugly face. The fact that she thought that nasty shit was funny, pissed me off more than words could express. I think the whore intentionally waited to tell Dre! When the doctor left the room I came back to reality. "Where is she going?" Dre looked at me very strange. "You didn't hear her, she went to get another doctor to consult with." Dre put his hand on the top of mine and said I'm sorry. Frankly I was tired of the sorry song, I didn't want to hear it anymore! What was done was done, and that

Dre's payback was right in his face. He had to deal with his daughter being blind because of a dumb decision. Trina had to catch it because not only did she think it was funny, but she threw it in my face. Then on top of everything, she was in cahoots with Kalief! The doctor came back in the room with another pediatrician. That time I remained focus. After talking to Dr. Obdul I felt a whole lot better. She made me aware that it was possible to correct her sight. However that would be a decision that must be made soon.

"Dr. could you tell us more about the procedure first?" The doctor went on to explain to us about the surgery. My first impression was that getting the surgery was more dangerous than not. I wanted to do what was best for my baby but the surgery was not a guarantee. I looked at Dre with a confused look. "We have to try something."

Leaving the doctors office I felt a lot more optimistic. "Dre when we get home there's something I have to tell you." "Why you can't tell me now?" "Just trust me!" I said. "Aight, whateva you say." I cut my eye at Dre, rolling them, then turning my head. "Dre turn it down some,

Chapter Fifteen

I'm about to call mama." "Hey mama we just left the appointment."
"Yeah, and how did it go?" "It just went! Makya is blind in one eye
and possibly going blind in her other one." "SAY WHAT! Stacie not
my baby, what can they do for her?" "Mama baby girl is going in for
surgery in two weeks. They put her on steroids for these two weeks
to get her stronger. Dre is putting in for his family medical leave and
I'll have to take a leave of absence as well. "

"Do not forget me, you know I am here!" "I do Mama." "You know
what Stase, I think you should get a lawyer, because those doctors
at the first clinic should be held liable." Mama went on. "You have
all the proof you need, your baby is suffering because they didn't
inform you. Girl please you have a medical malpractice case." "Go
ahead Mama do it, and I'll call you in a bit." Mama was like a money
magnet she attracted it. I never saw anyone who didn't have a job but
stayed with cash but a hustler. Mama kept a pocket full of money.

"Dre do you think Kya will be okay?" "Stacie you have to have faith,
I believe she will be more than okay. Stacie do you remember the first
real time we talked? You told me you did not think your life was in
vein." "Yup." "Well keep believing that." "Thanks Dre that advice
was perfect." We took the babies in the house and got them situated.
It was time for me and Dre to have a heart to heart conversation.
The babies went down for a nap and me and Dre sat at the table
ready to conduct business.

"Aight Stacie what's up?" "Dre it's so much I don't know where to
begin. Dre we have to do something, you won't believe what I'm
about to tell you! Trina and Kalief are an item." "So what! Fuck
him and her forreal! His punk ass need to be in jail, what are we
gonna do about that?" "Dreeeeee, nooooo did you just hear what I
said? Baby Kalief only started messing with Trina after he started
following me. One day he sat in the cut and watched Trina make
a fool out of herself in the parking lot. She then became his meal
ticket. He lied to Trina and told her I was his ex.

"Dre it gets deeper. Kalief is still after me and he'll do just about
anything to get me." "Yo I can't believe what I'm hearing!" "That

prank phone calls. Dre something has to be done and it have to be done soon. I rather us go at them before they can strike first. I'm afraid if we don't set him up to go to jail I might be dead soon." "Man I will blow that bastards balls off. Now Stacie you know I'm not a violent person, but I will hurt him! Stase this is real talk, I tried to be the up right guy and do the right thing but enough is enough! The police aren't doing shit! I tell you what, that dude betta not cross my path, Ima blow his ass off this earth."

I had Dre right where I wanted and needed him, mad as hell! It was about damn time because some new shit was about to pop off. Dre never even asked me how I knew all of that. He was always so nice, naive, and gullible. That day I saw a side of him that I never saw before. I was waiting for my Clyde before I put my Bonnie suite on. For about two hours Dre and I sat up and put together a plan that would put Davon's ass in jail and I would get the golden opportunity to whoop Trina's ass. But the timing was crappy, that was my major problem. It all had to go down before Kya's surgery. I guess with everything going on, Dre felt the need to share some things with me as well. "Stacie after this is all over will you think about being a full time mother until the kids are about two." I looked at Dre like he was insane.

"Here me out before you turn me down Stacie. I can cover all the bills plus some. I can take good care of you and the babies. Stacie when the kids get about two or three you can go to school if you like. But right now they need you." "Dre I here you and I love the fact that you are willing to work like a dog to provide for us but babe we need you home too. I rather both of us bring in income so you won't have to work so much. If you are working like a dog to provide then we will hardly see you." Dre said nothing he just pulled out a bank statement The bank statement primary account holder was Dre, there right under his name was mine. That part blew me away. I think it was the balance that did it for me more. The balance was well over forty-two thousand. Where in the hell did you get this had lead so every so often I get partial settlement." My mouth hit the floor. "Dam I could of got two pair of Uggs!" I said laughing. "Huh, you don't listen, I told you to get what you wanted. Stacie I ordered your card it should be here next week."

Chapter Sixteen

Mama had to be aware of what was going on. Knowing her, she would be the one who kept the kids while it went down. However, part of the plot was happening a bit too close to mama's house. Dre and I agreed that she and the kids should go to the hotel until it was all over. It was just a safety precaution. The plan was in motion. "Stacie what day do you want me to say?" "Let's do it Saturday, that way we know for sure that mama and the babies are safe." "Alright cool." "Ummm, Dre what the hell are you doing?" "Calling Trina!" "Hell no! Not off your cell phone! C'mon Dre use that brain!" He laughed then said dam, "You right! See that's why you are my girl!" We drove to the nearest pay phone which was at the K-mart up the street from the house.

"Hello!" "Trina this Dre wussup?" "Dre! And why are you calling me?" "Trina you were right, I want to be with you! This thang between me and Stacie is not working out! Besides I miss you Trina." "Whateva Dre, so you think I'm coming back to play step mommy! Are you serious?" Trina said. "Anyway you too late I have moved and I am happy now.

I could tell whatever Trina just said pissed Dre off some kind of bad. I rubbed his arm so he would keep his cool. "Aight, I hear you forget it!" I smacked his arm. Simultaneously, then she must of changed her mind. "When do you want to see me Dre?" "What are you doing Saturday?" "What time?" Trina asked. "Can you meet me around alright Dre whateva!" Click......She hung up.

"Aright Stase, so when will I know to call the police?" Dre you're gonna have to call me. I'm quite sure he'll be close by. Think about it, what made her change her mind so fast! The same way I hit your arm, Kalief was probly right there too. What I will do is keep my Bluetooth in my ear under my hair, so when you call I can get it."

That Friday we spent quality time as a family. We took the babies to the safari drive in. It was more fun for me and Dre. The kids didn't no what the heck was going on! I gave mama a fly hair do before her boyfriend came and took them to the hotel. I would have took them but I couldn't chance Kalief following me. Even though we planned it out, the pit of my stomach said something could still go wrong. At that point there was no turning back. I was in it to win it. I knew that if we didn't do something fast it could come back and bite us in the bottom. Around ten o'clock I got ready for bed. I left Dre up playing madden. It was cool with me because I had to sleep off the nerves.

Saturday morning I woke up to the clock saying 9:36. Dre was in the kitchen cooking up this big breakfast. Bacon, French toast, cheese eggs, and a fruit bowl. "Dam!" I said to myself. I didn't have much of an appetite. As I Drove down Sinclair lane my heart was pounding. I don't know why, Trina wasn't to big for my britches. I could handle that ass by all means. I pulled up in the complex lot. I parked on the other side. This way I could see who was coming in and who was leaving out. No one could see inside the Volvo because of the tents. I sat there for about twenty minutes. My short patients was running out. Finally an unknown car pulled into the lot. A few seconds later, there she was stepping out on the drivers side.

"Dre I will call you back, here she go." And that freak said she wasn't pressed! I couldn't tell it was mid December by the way she was dressed. Her stank behind had on a mini skirt and some open toe boots. I had on boots too but they damn sure wasn't open toed. As she walked toward the car I unlocked the doors. She was familiar expected her to come to the passenger side and get in. My adrenaline was pumping and my thoughts were all tangled up. Catching me off guard she came to the drivers side. I knew if I rolled down the window the plan wasn't going to work, I had to think fast. Her intentions weren't to ever get in. I swung the door open as she got close to it. When the door opened it smacked her knees and made that ass buckle! I jumped out with my Nike boots and sweats on and went to work. Not the plan at all! At least not like that.

All of Trina's body was everywhere. She couldn't catch her balance because of those ugly boots. That gave me every thing I needed to keep whooping her tail. The plan was basically going down the drain. I was wondering why Dre never called me back. "Bitch you thought it was funny!" I screamed at her. "My baby is sick because of your stank ass!" Kicking her in her ribs one last time before I took a lethal blow to her head. That punch knocked me off my feet. When I realized it was another broad coming my way I panicked. The plan was out of the window. Trina got up and her and the other chick charged me. "Screw that I am not going out like this!" I told myself.

I jumped up head ringing and all. What those broads didn't know was that, I was about to hurt one of them! Trina home girl came bucking and when she went to swing that was her last one. My blade met her face and that skin filleted like a fish. By then I had snapped! As Trina approached me she didn't even realize I had cut her girl. So as she approached me she got it too. But with Trina I never let go. It was like I went into a trance. I grabbed her and started stabbing her and stabbing her. By the time I had come to, I had stabbed her over ten times. I heard somebody say, call the police. It was probably the home girl, but I didn't give a care. It all happened so fast. When I heard that, I ran back to the Volvo. As I was running I heard a car slam on the breaks.

Never looking back I just kept running. Before I could get to the car I could hear Trina saying Lief, Lief! I was out of breath, and my legs because that was apart of the plan. To get his ratchet face behind bars! It was never in the plan for me to be behind bars too. I don't know if it was fear or anger that made me do it!

When I heard Trina talking to Kalief I never heard him say anything back. Then I heard the footsteps coming after me. I wasn't afraid of that because that was apart of the plan. I just hoped the end of the plan played out. I never intended on hurting anybody like I did. In my mind, I knew deep down that me and Trina would fight, but I didn't expect it to go that far, for me to stab her. Far as Kalief he was suppose to chase me but in his car!

"Dam I'm out here caught in BS, what about my kids!" I thought to myself as I fumbled around for the keys. I guess I should of thought of a better plan huh. As I stumbled with the keys I forgot to lock the car doors. Kalief coming after me was the plan, him jumping in my backseat was not! "Drive BITCH!" "Where we going?" I said. Thank goodness it was Dre calling. My phone was on vibrate and my hair and hat covered my earpiece in my ear. Kalief was confused himself, he did not know what to say.

I hit the answer button on the Bluetooth and said, "Kalief where are we going? Do the cat got cha tongue?" "Bitch shut up!" "I should blow you away right now!" "Where, here on Bowleys lane!" That was my way of letting Dre know where I was at. "Where dat punk ass boyfriend of yours at?" "Who Dre, he's probly home wondering where I'm at!" I said sarcastically. "Let's go home den!" Kalief said. "Right then Dre felt the need to speak. "Stase stop being slick at the mouth before he kill you, bring his ass to me!" Dre said. Damn his plan was better than ours. "Bring em to daddy." Dre said, in my ear once again. I tried to play it off so he wouldn't expect anything. I knew Dre heard him so the unmarked cars should be waiting on us upon arrival.

"C'mon Kalief leave my family out of this, it's between me and you." "Those were the last words Davon said to me." Kalief said calmly.

time. He left me in that hotel room and then he started selling weight and didn't even cut me in! All those years we survived together and then you came along and took my best friend away. AND WHAT THE FUCK IS YOU DRIVING SO SLOW FOR?" Kalief yelled. "Home sweet home." I said through my teeth so only Dre could hear me. After I said that the phone hung up. Dre probably hung up to call them boys.

Although the plan was totally screwed on my part, I didn't mind paying the consequences. Hopefully I could get off on self defense. I'm pretty sure Trina would rat me out. Either way I knew I was going down. At least I knew he would survive financially. Plus since Dre showed me the bank statement, I knew he could afford a lawyer and my bail. Things always went sour for me! The good things I did end up going wrong, so I didn't know why I expected a plan that involves me whooping ass could go good.

I slowly whipped the Volvo in the parking lot, and I realized that all the cars there, I knew. "What the hell!" I know Dre got the damn clue I said to myself. Slowly we walked toward the apartment building. I had a gun stuck to my side and Kalief's dirty ass arm was around my neck. I immediately started praying. Life couldn't be more screwed up than it was at that moment! Once we climbed the last flight of steps I started coughing so Dre could hear me.

Kalief pushed the gun into my side telling me to shut up. I played around with the keys giving Dre yet another sign. Kalief said, "You can never imagine what it was like for me to loose my friend, but now I will give you the opportunity to know exactly what it's like. Its your turn, Dre's a dead man!" The door opened and my body went numb. I didn't know what was about to happen! I was crying for Dre on the inside. "Please Dre......please baby be ready." In my heart something told me to trust Dre.

I finally opened the door. When I realized the apartment door wouldn't open all the way I caught on. Before I could step all the turn around and I jumped across the room. BOOM! Kalief never made it all the way around. His body dropped lifelessly. I got up to see Dre standing there with the gun still pointed in Kalief's direction. I also saw his phone in the other hand as he dialed 911.

The gun was like a master piece, it was so huge. It sure wasn't the one we practiced with. "Dreee what! what!" I didn't know what to say. The plans on both of our end had been altered. Kalief laid there with a bullet in his head bleeding everywhere. Dre was totally messed up. What neither one of us knew was that the police were on their way, even before Dre called them. Before I left the parking lot at mama's apartment complex someone retrieved the information on the Volvo. They were coming for me anyway. Dre put the gun on the table just as nice. He then came and hugged the life out of me. "It's enough money to hold yall down for a while, take care of the kids. I also think it's a good idea for you to file that law suite like Ms. Lisa

"No this can't be happening! Tell me this is a bad dream!" I cried. "I'm going to jail, Dre I stabbed Trina, they were about to bank me and I panicked!" Dre stood back and looked at me. Then the police banged on the door. "Open up police!" Not moving the gun off of the table or nothing Dre went right to the door. The police came like ten deep. "We are here for two reasons I see." The officer said. One officer looked at me and started questioning me about driving Dre's car. I told her I went to my mama's house and they banked me and I was scared for my life. That's when I was held at gunpoint and was forced to drive home by Kalief.

The officer said that Dre would be home in a matter of hours because Kalief had crossed his threshold. When Kalief came in, that gave him every right to protect himself. His ride was just for a statement and filing paperwork. The officer then said some words that I will never forget. We have to take you in for the murder of Katrina Bonds. They placed the cuffs on me and read me my rights. Dre's face read eyes filled with tears. My eyes also watered and my knees buckled. The officer caught me then lifted me up. Dre looked at me and told me not to say anything, to just wait for the lawyer to arrive. I shook my head up and down, I didn't even have the guts to look him in the eyes anymore. Two people that had been played with too many times were being screwed again. That time it was the choices that we made. I must have blacked out because I couldn't remember stabbing her over twenty times. The report stated that I stabbed her 22 times. With each draw of my hand I pictured a different incident in my life.

Chapter Seventeen

Basically things happened for Dre just like the officer said it would. Thank God he didn't spend a day in jail. For me, murder was the case that they gave me. (In my Snoop Dogg voice). Dre kept his word, as soon as he came home, he got on the horn to an attorney. Steve Snyderback was there before the end of the day. Dre had already told him what happened but as my attorney he had to hear it from me. At first he was hell bent on using the self defense mechanism. But when he realized how many times I stabbed her he knew that was out the window. However, once he went over everything he decided to go with the self defense and temporary insanity plea. At that time, it was only one year ago that I endured such trauma. He planned to use that to my advantage as well. The whole rape, murder thing. PTSD, Post traumatic stress disorder was the correct diagnosis.

Once again I made the headlines of the local news. This time instead of the victim I was the guilty villain. They linked both stories together so initially I still had a small pity party. Dre didn't get a chance to call mama and tell her what was going on before she saw it on the news.

I wondered about Mama at times. What kind of damn person sit in a five star hotel watching the news! Then I found out that she only cut the news on after her neighbor called her and told her what had happened. The neighbor claimed to have been worried about me, and she knew mama was away for the weekend. "Dre come get me!"

"Dre I don't want to hear anything just come and get me! Stanley left and I want to know what happened, so come on!" "Alright I'm on my way."

Our apartment was still a crime scene. Dre cancelled the football game that he had scheduled. Dre didn't mind getting Mama, it was the twins he worried about. He did not know how he was going to pull it off without me there. After letting Dre and the babies in the apartment, Mama went over to her home girl, Miss Bunny's apartment. Dre felt awkward about everything. Instead of driving the Volvo he drove my car. When mama came back she had some good news for Dre.

"Dre listen I need you to get in touch with Stacie's lawyer. My girlfriend Bunny is willing to testify on Stacie's behalf. Now I hope the states attorney don't get a whole rack of witnesses to go against what Bunny says. Bunny is willing to hoodwink the story to benefit Stacie, you wit me!" "Yeah I hear you." Although Dre agreed, he knew that it wouldn't be that easy. Dre made the necessary calls to contact the lawyer. The lawyer was very pleased with everyone's effort to help. He agreed to meet with Mama, Miss Bunny, and Dre after my bail review on Monday.

The miscommunication between Dre and I was unsettling. I know he was probably thinking I lied to him. I couldn't imagine what was going through his mind. I had too much time to think, I hoped he didn't think I used him. Then, to have to mourn for Trina was another thing. They may had split up, but that didn't erase their long history together. He was just trying to prove to me that he really did love me and he was going to do whatever it took. When I finally talked to him I could hear exactly how he felt. I could hear the hurt in his voice.

That Sunday when I was allowed to make my phone call, I called Dre. "You have a collect call from, Stacie. If you would like to except here. Dre we don't have that long to talk so let me get this all in. Dre I did not intend for this to happen. I am sorry that I killed her Dre, I got scared! I never used you to kill her things just didn't go as planned. I promise it was an accident." "Stacie stop, you might think I'm mad at you, but I'm not. The mother of my children is locked up for murder. A murder that she was pushed into!" "No Dre, I had a choice!" "Stase I didn't keep my end of the bargain either. But Stacie I didn't keep mine intentionally." Dre said. "Stacie night after night I sat there and watched you have nightmare after nightmare. I told myself if I ever had the opportunity to lay that motherfucker down I was gonna do just that. Far as Trina is concerned, of course I wish things would have went different. I wish she would have left us alone and maybe she would still be alive. But what's done is done!" Hidden Resentment, Bolding Page/ 196

"Girl I love you, so stop doubting that. I'm gonna ride this thing out with you I promise!" I heard the thirty second warning beep. " Dre I love you too babe, but the call is ready to end. How are the kids?" "They're fine." "Ok good, I'll see you tomorrow." "Yeah your bail review, what time is it?" "Ten!" Click........the phone hung up. I wanted to cry so bad. When I looked around and saw all the roughneck chicks I sucked them tears right up!

The next morning before my bail review I met with my lawyer. He came in so perky. I can admit I wasn't in his spirits. I was afraid I wasn't going to make bail for my baby's surgery. When I told the lawyer that I was just venting, I never knew he would use that to my defense to get me a bail. You rarely hear of a murderer out on bail. The judge bought it, but my bail was darn ridiculous. The judge set the bail for one million dollars. My eyes got big as hell! I looked back at Dre's expression and his matched mine. Mama on the other hand, she looked pretty confident. I read Mama's lips which read, I got you. I thought to myself, what in the world is Mama talking about? Did she know what million dollars was? "That's it, I'm stuck!"

Seeing Trina's ugly ass face and seeing Kalief's blood trail to my shoes. My future was screwed and I knew it. Although Trina and Kalief were both dead I shared not an ounce of remorse. I was cold, bitter, and I hated it! I felt sorry for the kids, but I knew that they would be okay because they had Mama and Dre. There was no way I was getting out of here. I was tired of my life; I didn't even understand why I was still here.

Three days in and I had given up hope. I was about to make my cell my home, the gates opened for breakfast. For a while I had thrown myself a pity party, finally I said enough. I said forget it, I might as well get use to it. In the lunchroom sitting to the left of me was a group of dyke broads. I could hear them talking mad smack. I should of went with my first instinct, to stay my tail in my cell. I normally skipped breakfast, but that day was different.

"Yeah dats da bitch dat was on the news for stabbing shorty!" I thought to myself, she wasn't no damn shorty! Her ass was about as tall as Kobe! I couldn't feed into their bull, they could say all they wanted and it wouldn't phase me. I know one thing for sure not one of them dyke bitches better not step! Normally I had no problem with what ones sexual preference was. However, don't try to intimidate me with it, because at the end of the day your Va-JJ bleed every month just like mine. I could not believe the chicks kept mouthing off. "Yeah like I thought you aint so tough without dat blade!" "Girl eff you!" I lashed back at her. Before I knew it her big ass was all over me. I didn't go out like a sucker though. I fought that big winch! In a blink of an eye I blacked out again. Her girlfriend used the end of a bobby pin and cut my face. The situation was so surreal. The guards came running in and broke it up. The guard asked for medical escort services over the radio. Those whores were fine, I didn't know what was going on. It wasn't until I felt the blood dripping from my face that I realize the medical escort was for me.

meals landing on my food, with their nasty ass. It seemed like then I was the one always getting hurt. By then I had so much anger and frustration inside, that I didn't mind unleashing it. In the nurse's suite, where I ended up getting my face glued and bandaged up, I cried. I cried so much. I missed my babies, I missed Dre and mama, but once again, I wasn't sure I could move on. The nurse took pity on me and gave a little pep talk.

"Stacie's your name right." "Yes." I said sobbing. "Stacie I want you to pull yourself together! Whatever it is your going through, remember it will not last forever. Behind every test there is a testimony. Stacie, to get to, you must go through. The good Lord won't put more on you than you can bare. Give all of your problems and worries to God. One last thing, you must change your mind set. Don't be so negative about everything, fighting is not the answer. If you stay positive, God will fight your battles for you. It's not to late!"

Everything the nurse said sounded good but I didn't know how to apply it to my life. "I grew up parentless, became homeless, sold drugs for a living, got raped, beaten, and saw Davon get killed. Back tracking, we found my Aunt Tina in the house dead, and I stole everything I had. Fast forwarding, I had twins by two different fathers. My girls eye sight was affected by a nasty ass STD, and now I am facing murder among other bullshit charges. It all add up to me being taken away from the only pure part of my life, my babies." "You listen to me, hold on because God has something good for you! Don't give up baby, begin by praying." The door opened and two woman guards came in. "Stacie McCall you made bail." For that quick moment I got happy. The nurse gave me a hug, which was truly against the rules. After that I was out of there. When the guards opened the gates and I saw Dre standing there I was rushed with an overwhelming feeling. In spite of my face having a big bandage on it I felt blessed. I ran to Dre with opens arms. Dre extended his arms right back.

eva let me go!" Dre laughed and said you got it! Dre cuffed my booty as he put me down. "I see that didn't change!" Dre said. "I heard that!" Mama said, getting out of the car. " Maaaa, my family, where's the babies? Mama looked at me like I was crazy and said, "Stase you aint gonna believe where they at! Well, let me take that back, they are at my place, but guess with who....Shalese!" Mama said. "For real mama, I can't believe yall!" I looked at Dre and gave him a funny face. "My babies better be okay!" I said laughing. "Stacie what happen to your face?" Mama asked with much concern. Nothing gets pass her big eyes! "I was fighting and a girl cut my face." "Well dag, Stacie you said that like you don't care!" "Look Mama it aint like that, over the past few years I been to hell and back! Certain things I have to accept and other things I need to change, I know that! I know I cannot change nothing in my past, even what took place a few hours ago. But I can say this, I will change my future!" Dre looked at me and gave me an approving smile. "You go girl," Mama said. "Stase is the cut bad?" Dre asked. "It's not as bad as it could of been." Right then I felt a change of heart coming over me. A whole new meaning of life suddenly came over me.

Chapter Eighteen

The lawyer was on his A game! I mean he was great at what he do! Going before the judge looked like a piece of cake. He had his arguments, opening and closing statements. The judge that we went before was the typical power struck judge. Snyderback wasn't a fan of him. The judge was definitely zero tolerance. The district attorney offered me forty years. The evidence my attorney produced seemed to be more than enough to get my sentence reduce. The witness alone, I thought did the job.

Each day of the trial was more draining than the one before. The forty year sentence wasn't going anywhere so my attorney motioned for a jury trial. Even the jury seemed like they had it in for me. There reasonable doubt against me was the fact that I could of walked away. If it was self defense it should not taken me to the twenty second time for me to get away. Trina's life should have been spared. They saw nothing through my eyes. Maybe my attorney was right, maybe I was suffering from a post traumatic stress disorder, temporary insanity even. The verdict was in.

"On the count of first degree murder we the jury find the defendant Stacie McCall, Guilty. On the count of second degree assault with a deadly weapon, we the jury find the defendant, guilty." The jury found me guilty on every single charge. I was good and gone. 19 years old with a set of one year old twins, GONE!

I hope you learn a very valuable lesson while serving your time. I am sentencing you to forty years in a maximum state institution with the possibility of parole after 15 years served." Then the gavel banged. I closed my eyes and thought about what the nurse said, and for once in my life I did not cry nor was I angry. Although when I turned to look at Dre and Mama, their reaction said something totally different. Both of their eyes were filled with the liquid chemical known to man as tears. I had no more left in me. At least not sad ones. I thought to myself, the next time I cried it would be for a joyous occasion. The new chapter in my life was about to begin.

Three months had gone past and like clock work I saw Dre and the kids every Wednesday. Mama and Shalese came on Fridays. While I was in there I had to make the best of it. I tried the whole thinking positive thing. I figured if I could make parole in fifteen years than I would still get to see my kids graduate from school high. Being locked up, made me mentally tougher. I stopped feeling sorry for myself. There were girls with more devastating stories than mine. The girls around me started feeding off of my positive energy, I became a leader. On my tier the fights reduced, and most of us became hungry for education and wisdom that only came from above. Before I knew it, teaching and counseling was apart of my sentencing. After about six months in prison I faced the truth. That next Wednesday I asked Dre to leave the kids with Mama and come see me. I told him that he deserved to be happy. I let him know it was okay to move on with his life. I just wanted him to be a good daddy.

"Dre eventually she'll be right there in your face, and when that happens I want you to be able to make clear decisions." "Stacie I don't want her I want you, you got that! Matter of fact who the hell is she?" "She is whoever she might be! Get my kids a good step mom. I'm not saying that it has to be right away, but I want you to let me go and move on. Dre I will always love you and if it's meant to be then it will be. For now do what's best for you and the babies.

on the case and he went back to fighting mold. I think the advice the nurse gave me was the best thing I had ever heard. Applying it to my life changed it for the better. Since I began to focus on positive things and left the past behind, everything around me had a positive energy. This might sound crazy, but even the tier I was on was peaceful. Because of the peace and quiet time, I was able to start writing in my journal. I get it now, I think. I often wondered if I had not done what I done, would life still be the same. Would Trina still be harassing us or would Kalief still be alive. I never knew God was so good. Maybe if I prayed and tried a little more, he would have fought all of my battles. Now I had to pay the price for taken a life. One who wasn't even the cause of my demise. It was me, I caused my own demise. Unfortunately she caught me at a transition point of my life. No excuse but it is the truth. Baby girl's surgery was a major success. My baby had full sight. Mama told me how rough the first two weeks were for them but thereafter, mama said she was running around getting into everything.

Mama loved every bit of it. I feel the need to let a little secret out of the bag. Lisa gave birth to me at the age of thirteen. I had the twins at eighteen. It's not hard to figure out how old Mama is. Awe the hell with it, I'll just tell it! Mama was only thirty two years old. That's why it was so easy for me to forgive her and move on. Because of her innocent age when she had me, I can only imagine how frightening that was. Me and Mama are more like friends now even to this day. The twins were a fresh start for both of us. Shalese became fed up with her father's mess and moved with Mama. Now Mama is talking about getting Cal out to live with her too.

Dre......Hmmm, what can I possibly say about that man. He would not give up. Mama had me laughing. She said she was surely keeping Lese hot behind away from Dre! She said that wasn't happening on her watch. I laughed so hard. Dre finally moved into a three bedroom townhouse in the Whitemarsh area. He even paid Mama's first month rent and security deposit so she could move next door.

development and Dre hopped on the opportunity. It was smart if you ask me. Basically he will always have a baby sitter. The twin lawsuit was into play. Mama said so far so good. Because of their high risk of negligence and liability their lawyer even advised them to settle out of court. They didn't want to but that was being negotiated. If I can say so myself, through each incident, there was a lesson to be learned. The first lesson was to make the best of any situation because life was too short. In a blink of an eye, change can and will consume your life.

In all things we reap what we sow. So I have learned to treat people the way I want to be treated. Even in negative situations try to stay positive. Positive thoughts equal positive results. Last but not least on the list is forgiveness. If there is someone in your life who you love dearly and they have wronged you, Forgive them! Forgive them! It's a hard lesson, but trust me, it's one to make your life much better. Don't hold on to your past but visualize your brighter future. I had to stop playing the blame game too. I was so quick to blame everybody else for my mucked up life, and I do mean mucked up! Had I made better choices, things would have been different. Oh well what can I say we live and we learn.

Chapter Nineteen

Things were beginning to really be great between Dre and I before all of the madness. Somehow I couldn't help but to wonder if he could really wait for me. Of course I wanted him to wait, but how selfish would that be. The judge didn't say four years, he said forty years. The way Mama tell it, the kids have Dre quite occupied. She made it her business to tell me how the twins kept everybody busy. Thinking about Makai and Kya I wish I would have gotten counseling, because before now I never took responsibility for my own actions. I wasn't in any shape to judge anybody. I played the victim every time. Something that I was so good at doing. That was a lifestyle that I had given into. Now my anger, that shit could have been hereditary. Because getting to know Mama, her butt is crazy too! Not only did I follow in her footsteps with the stabbing, but I let all of that built up anger consume me.

I started out resilient and steadfast but the ultimate decision I made cost me my life. I was alive but not able to live. When the judge banged the gavel and sentenced me to forty years that was the second time in my life that I seen it flash before my eyes. It would take this for Dre to have no choice and be by himself. He did have the twins so technically he wasn't alone, but time without a woman was good. Mama now had two babies and a niece. It's amazing how the tables magnet baby girl won a healthy lawsuit. Thank God Mama was still young, she could handle every bit of it. The twins were in good hands. What I regret the most about my actions is that the saga continued for my babies not having mommy around. Luckily I was highly favored by the higher power. That letter of appeal that I received, definitely came from the higher power. The appeal went through. My new sentence was seven years, with two years time served and the other five years was probation. The five years probation was the judges idea. He heard about how I had great effect on the girls in the prison facility. So he made me go weekly to different youth facilities and motivate young woman. Plus it was a glitch in the first trial that made it that much easier for my sentence to be overturned. Now this I can live with. Remember to face all challenges with faith and confidence. Let us not be our own worse nightmares.